Leonardo's Hand

Leonardo's Hand

by Wick Downing

Houghton Mifflin Company
Boston 2001

To my three sons, Phillip, Paul, and John, who as children were compelled to suffer through the adventures of Walter QuickerWalkie and other experiments.

Library of Congress Cataloging-in-Publication Data

Downing, Warwick, 1931–
Leonardo's hand / Wick Downing.
p.   cm.
Summary: Finally in a foster home with a caring family, Nard, a thirteen-year-old orphan with only one hand, invents a human-powered flying machine with the assistance of the 500-year-old hand of Leonardo da Vinci.
ISBN 0-618-07893-2
[1. Orphans—Fiction. 2. Physically handicapped—Fiction. 3. Foster home care—Fiction. 4. Inventions—Fiction. 5. Leonardo, da Vinci, 1452–1519—Fiction.] I. Title.
PZ7.D7595 Le 2001   [Fic]—dc21   00-032034

Manufactured in the United States of America
QUM 10 9 8 7 6 5 4 3 2 1

Acknowledgments

Some writers, I have heard, are like Mozart. They have heard the song in their heads before writing it and are able to spin out the melody with confident ease, knowing it can't be improved upon.

I would love to be one of them, but I am not. My songs, the first time they are written, are painfully dull. Some of them have promise, but at the beginning they are not much more than the glimmer of an idea that is in serious need of help.

This book was like that. Had I not had the good luck to join a group of writers, many of whom are published authors, who call themselves the Wild Women Writers of the West, and a Few Good Guys, this tale would never have become publishable.

I am one of the guys. The women in the group, and another guy, endured several tedious beginnings without too much complaint, criticizing and cajoling and tweaking the tale into something that was not too much of an embarrassment. They were brutal at times, hilarious at others, but constant in one regard: they were encouraging.

My grateful thanks to each of you: Julie Ann Peters, Hilari Bell, Anna Maria Crum, Ann Sullivan, Caroline Stutson, Carol Crowley, Shawn Shea, Meridee Cecil, Bobbi Shupe, Coleen DeGroff, and Lili Bell Shelton. These people aren't just wild, incidentally. They are totally out of control.

I also wish to thank my agent, Sally Brady, for her criticisms, suggestions, and help; and Amy Flynn, my gentle and wonderfully supportive editor at Houghton Mifflin.

One

"Nard? Are you up there?"

My caseworker calling. I recognized her voice but couldn't see her. I was in my "summer place," which is what I call the wastewater culvert above the Cherry Creek bike path.

It's cool there in the summer, but this was April and there were still patches of snow in the shade. That's how it is in Colorado in the spring. I could even see my breath.

"Hi, Mrs. Cousins." I'd zipped up my coat and pulled my wool hat over my ears, then stretched out on a platform made of scrap wood. It hung between the curved walls of the culvert and kept me dry. A thin trickle of water slid along the bottom, out the mouth. "How did you find me?"

"This is the third time, Nard. You can't stay there."

Don't thirteen-year-old orphans have any rights? Three days ago I'd run away from a foster home placement, barely escaping with my life. "I'm better off here, Mrs. Cousins. Really."

"What if it rains? Or worse, what if it snows again?"

"I'm not worried. The rainfall average in Eldorado for April is 1.7 inches, and we got that a week ago."

"Please, Nard. Don't make me call the police."

"You don't have to call them if you don't want to." I scooched forward and peered down on her. When she looked up at me it stretched her face, pulling the wrinkles out. "Don't send me back there. You don't know what that old man was like."

"How do you get up there?" she asked. "I mean, without a ladder. Do you pull it up behind you?"

The culvert is like a cave in a cliff. I get there from the street level down. What made it safe was that no one else had figured out how to do it. "You have to be able to fly."

It was pretty out, even if it was cold. Cherry Creek splashed along on the other side of the bike path, and the grass on its banks had greened up. Some willows along the edge had tiny leaves.

"I'm sorry about that placement, Nard. Was it awful?"

"*She* was okay, but *he* was into training. Reveille in the morning. Inspections. I had to salute him." I laughed even though it wasn't funny. "When I messed up, he put me in a doghouse. A real doghouse."

"Duck," she said. A couple of cyclists approached, and I yanked my face out of the way. "It's okay," she said, after they whizzed by.

I stuck my head back out. She really was on my side, or she wouldn't care if someone saw me up there. She wanted to find me a good home, too. But the foster home market in Eldorado had dried up; plus I was a challenge. I was born without a left hand, and a deformity like that grosses people out. I'm also smarter than most people, which pisses them off.

"What am I going to do with you?" she asked.

"Adopt me."

"Believe me, I've thought about it," she said. "Would you consider a pig farm?"

"Pig farm! Like out in the country?"

"The suburbs, actually. Do you know where Bergen Lake is?"

"Is there a pig farm out there?" It was twenty-five miles out of town and surrounded by rich people in mansions. But pig farms are like factories that make pigs. They create huge amounts of waste products, stink like sewers, and draw flies.

"It isn't one of those big commercial operations," she said. "The woman who owns it has roots in Colorado. Her great-grandfather homesteaded the farm way back in the 1800s."

A pig farm with a history would still be a pig farm, I thought. The prospect of living on one didn't interest me.

3

"I don't think so, Mrs. Cousins. I'm kind of a city orphan. I need a downtown fix on a fairly regular basis."

"Would you consider it? She... well, she needs the money."

Foster parents have to fill out forms to show their suitability. They lie a lot. "You mean, where it says 'give reasons,' she put 'for the money' or something like that?"

"Yes."

"She didn't say 'Because I love children and want to provide a caring environment for some poor youngster in need'?"

"All she said was, 'Money.'"

Different, at least. "I'll think about it."

Mrs. Cousins pulled a bill out of her purse and hid it under a rock. "It's two o'clock," she said. "Get something to eat and clean up. I'll be back at four."

One advantage orphans have over other kids is that they aren't burdened with possessions. Except for what I had on, everything I owned was in my backpack. An almanac, a dictionary, some extra clothes, a toothbrush, and a comb. Mrs. Cousins had left me five dollars to clean up with. I spent a dollar fifty at the laundromat on Pearl on clothes, washing and drying all of them, even the ones I was wearing. I wrapped up in an old tattered bath towel somebody had left behind, then locked myself in the bathroom and washed up before putting the clean ones on. I looked kind of nerdy, but my hair was combed and I didn't smell.

Two tacos from Taco Billy's, one candy bar, and a large orange juice with no ice took $3.42. I had a nickel and three pennies to jingle in my pocket.

Mrs. Cousins was right on time. "Hi," she said, smiling at me and testing the air with her nose. "You don't look like you've been sleeping in a culvert. You look nice."

A big lie, but what can you expect from a social worker? "Thanks for the loan," I said, putting the pack on. "That's twenty-five dollars I owe you."

"You don't need to keep track of that!"

She led the way to her car. "Yes I do. Some day I'll pay you back."

It was evening rush hour. It would take an hour to drive the twenty-five miles to Bergen Lake, but I didn't care. It wasn't often I got to ride around in a car. With the window open, the wind felt good on my face. "What's her name?" I asked.

"Anna Swedenborge. A bit of a character, apparently."

"What does that mean?"

"You'll see."

Once off the freeway we drove past two golf courses, two shopping malls, through some residential suburbs and finally into farmland and countryside. We were aimed at the mountains west of Eldorado. Big slabs of rock called the "Flatirons" tilted up like shields protecting purple mountain ranges and snow-covered peaks in the distance. They floated above the horizon like islands in the sky with white jagged clouds drifting over them.

A sign said "Bergen Lake Estates. Private Drive." We didn't turn in there, though. We took a back entrance to get to the Swedenborge farm. It circled around behind the lake until the pavement ran out. "We're getting close," she said.

It felt like we were going back in time. A narrow dirt road turned off the main dirt road and we took it. We were like on the Depression Era side of the lake. The countryside was sagebrush and wire fences, and the shoreline was tall reeds and marshy where it met the water. Across the lake were big green lawns and boathouses in front of mansions and castles.

We drove toward an old wooden farmhouse that needed a paint job. So did the big barn and what I figured were pigpens. As we got closer I could smell them. The odor wasn't enough to make me sick, but it definitely stuck to my nose. "I don't know, Mrs. Cousins," I said. "What are my options?"

She squinted at me and shrugged. "Juvenile hall?"

Two

Mrs. Cousins drove into a dirt yard where clumps of yellow grass tried to grow. She parked next to a battered red pickup truck, between the barn and an old screen porch that hung off the back of the house. I left my pack in her car. We walked up wooden steps that creaked to a rickety screen door with patches in it, and she knocked. A girl, a little taller than me, came out of the house and onto the porch. "Hello," she said, suspiciously. She didn't open the door.

"Hi," Mrs. Cousins said. "Are you Julie?"

"Yes."

"I'm Mary Cousins from the Department of Social Services. Is your mother here?"

"I don't have a mother," Julie said, but walked toward us across the porch. "My Aunt Anna is..."

"Right behind you," another voice piped in. "Howdy do."

An old lady wearing denim pants, a baseball cap, and a canvas apron had come around the side of the house. She wiped her hands off on the apron, trotted up the steps, and stuck a hand out to Mrs. Cousins. "Pleased to meet you. We might could be more comfortable on the porch if I could get that girl to open the door."

"My Aunt Anna," Julie said, rolling back her eyes and opening the door. She had long black hair in a ponytail, dark eyes, and looked like she took things seriously.

"This must be the young man you was tellin' me about," the woman said to Mrs. Cousins. "What's your name?" she asked me. Her face kind of crinkled when she looked at me with blue eyes that locked on mine.

It felt like I was being searched, but not by a cop. It was a friendly search, if there is such a thing. "Leonard Smith," I said. "Everybody calls me 'Nard.'"

We shook hands. Hers was so tough and hard I thought I might get splinters. "What grade are you in at school?"

I swallowed and looked at Julie. "Seventh."

"That's fine. Julie...you met Julie?"

"Kind of."

"She's a seventh grader too. You'd ride the bus together I expect, if you was to live here. Was you in an accident?"

Her question caught me by surprise until I realized she was asking about my disability. I raised my stub so she could see it better. Most people won't even look at it, kind of like there's nothing wrong. "No," I told her. "That's the way I came."

"You mean you was born like that?"

"Yes."

"Now why would God do that to a boy?"

"Auntie, do you have to ask him that?" Julie asked.

"How else will I find out what kind of a boy he is?" She grinned. "He seems right nice to me. What do you think, Julie?"

Julie kind of gasped. "This is too weird," she said, staring at the floor.

I felt like a used car Anna might buy if it checked out. She kind of walked around me, kicking the tires. I liked her. It flashed on me that when people buy horses, they check their teeth. "Want to see my teeth?" I asked, showing them to her.

She laughed. So did Mrs. Cousins. Finally Julie did, too. "You'll do fine," Anna declared. "'Long as you ain't afraid of a little work."

When Mrs. Cousins drove away I waved at her, feeling kind of strange. It would have been all right with me if she'd given me a hug, even though that's against the rules. I hoisted my backpack over a shoulder, put a grin on my face, and turned around. A motor spluttered in the distance, then settled into a noisy roar. "What's that?" I asked Julie, who waited for me on the porch.

"Auntie just started the tractor up."

"What for?"

"Spring planting," Julie said. "Come on. I'll show you where you'll stay and stuff."

I followed her across the porch into a big kitchen. We walked into a living room with big windows, to a wooden staircase on the back wall, leading to a hallway on the second floor. Julie opened the first door on the right. "Your room."

It was okay. A single bed under the window, a table with a small lamp, and a closet.

"Mine is down the hall," she said. "Aunt Anna is across from me, and my dad sleeps downstairs."

Her dad? Another drill sergeant?

"His name is Farley Marne and he's a brakeman on the railroad." She waited by the door while I tossed my pack on the bed. "I'm Julie Marne and Anna is my dad's aunt. You either love her or you hate her. I love her, even though she drives me crazy."

"Who hates her?" I shut the door and ran to catch up. Julie was already down the steps.

"The people who live on the lake. They think they're so special because they're rich. But they ruin things with their money."

"Really?"

"I'll show you." She marched me through the living room and onto the front porch. I could see the lake, beyond a big square of yellow lawn. The lake had a thick border of marsh, with reeds and cattails sticking up. An old wooden dock stuck like a thumb into the water. A rowboat was tied to the end of it. "See?"

"See what?"

"The other side of the lake."

Massive houses were scattered around on huge green lawns that looked like golf courses. Thick green grass came down to the shoreline. I looked at sand beaches and boathouses as big as Anna's farmhouse. "What am I supposed to see?"

"You don't get it, do you?"

"No."

"Follow me." She skipped off the steps of the porch to a flagstone path that crossed the lawn. It disappeared into willows and cattails, through marshy grass and onto a narrow boardwalk. It floated on shallow water and led to the dock with the rowboat. We walked out there. I saw more huge houses with gardens and lawns and beach and boathouses and cement docks high above the water. They circled all around the lake. At the north end, a speedboat ripped through the water, tossing spray into the air. "Look at that," Julie said with disgust.

It looked great to me. "What's wrong?"

"We can't even fish the lake. Auntie gets like driven off." She glared at me. "You don't understand, do you?"

"I...I guess not."

"That's the trouble. Nobody does."

Walking back, we went around the house instead of through it. An old wooden door, level with the ground, was next to the screen porch. "What's that?" I asked, pointing at it.

"The root cellar, kind of an outdoor basement, that goes under the house."

"What's it for?"

"To store things in winter where they won't freeze. Auntie cans a lot of food in the fall and keeps it there. Farmers used to keep roots there for spring planting. Want to see it?"

It looked like a great place for spiders. "No thanks."

"I'll show you the barn." We went inside. "A big waste of space, actually. The tractor and stuff stay in the back, through that door. Where we are is where the animals go, but we don't keep horses anymore." I could smell dust and straw on the dirt floor. "Just a milk cow and some hens. Auntie milks her, but I have to clean her stable. Yuk."

"It's big in here," I said, looking around. "Like a hangar for airplanes." There were six stalls. Five were empty, but a cow, in the first one we came to, ambled over with his mouth working. "What's his name?" I asked.

"Her. Veronica. Hen house," she said, pointing to a pile of cages stacked on top of each other. They all had big feathery birds inside. "They'd lay more eggs if we could keep them outside, but we have to lock them in here. The neighborhood kids like to traumatize them."

"What do they do?"

"They are so mean. They let the pigs out, cut the fence, throw dirt clods at the hens. Once they started a fire in the pasture, like the Klan or something."

"Why?" I asked.

"Because it's fun. Because we don't fit in their neighborhood. Their parents kind of egg them on, and the sheriff's department won't do anything about it. They say we have to catch them in the act. Like, with blood on their hands!"

We went back outside...to a different world. In the two minutes we'd been in the barn, the sun had dropped behind the mountains. But shafts of sunrays beamed into the sky and bounced off clouds over our heads, reflecting down. Everything was beautiful, even the weeds and wooden fence posts and what was left of an old wagon, out in a field. "Wow," I said. It was as though the world had been scrubbed with soap, or something that made it sparkle.

"Auntie says if *she* catches them in the act, there won't be enough left for the sheriff to arrest." She pointed to her left. "The pig pen. It smells awful, but you get used to it." She showed me the pigs, in a big yard with a chainlink fence around it, troughs along the edges, and sheds at the ends. I counted four big pigs and three little ones. "They're cute," Julie said, "but you don't want to get to know them."

"Why not?" A couple of them came up to us, their little tails wagging.

"The future for pigs is not great. They grow up to be pork chops. I like sheep better, even though they aren't as friendly." We walked over to a pasture with a rail fence around it and wire squares hanging off the rails. Five sheep were in a clump, near an open shed in the middle. "They aren't meals except sometimes. Mostly wool. You've got a mosquito."

When she said that, I felt him on my neck. I whacked at him with my stub and missed, naturally, as he flew off. Suddenly we were in a swarm of the bloodsuckers and I waved my arms around like a propeller. "Help!"

We ran for the screen porch where it was safe. "No wonder you missed," she said later. "You used the wrong hand. I mean, why don't you use your hand instead of—" She stopped talking and looked like she wished the subject hadn't come up.

I scratched the welt on my neck. "It feels natural to use my stub," I said. "Almost like there's a hand on it."

"It does?"

"A doctor told me I'd be a serious left-hander, if I had one."

"That's weird," she said. "Maybe there's a disembodied hand out there somewhere . . . I mean—" She shrugged. "Auntie says I talk too much."

"You mean, like looking for an arm?" I held up my stub. It felt like the hand that wasn't there was doing pantomime. It did a rabbit face with ears, then a bird with a beak, then morphed into a globe of the world. Julie couldn't see it and neither could I, but I felt it experimenting with itself. "What if he attached himself to me, but I couldn't control him? Like he had a mind of his own?"

"Then you could shoot your worst enemy and it wouldn't be your fault."

"Cool." I smiled. "Except I don't have any enemies."

"*I* do," Julie said. "Lend him to me."

Julie fixed dinner while Anna worked in the fields with the tractor. I was starved and wanted to help Julie in the kitchen, but one thing you learn as an orphan is, don't do anything except breathe unless you're asked. It takes time to find out what you can get away with.

But I spotted a book on the couch and took a chance on looking at it. It had gotten dark outside, and it's usually okay to turn on lights without knowing the rules. Not TV though. Also, don't sit in somebody's favorite chair. I found one that looked safe. It didn't face the boob tube, didn't have cushions, and had a reading lamp nearby. I turned on the lamp and started to read.

The title of the book was *Isadora*. It was a biography and the foreword summarized her life story. Man! She got strangled by her own scarf! I was soaking up the details when the screen door slammed and a monster with a lunch pail in one hand came through the door.

He was so big he didn't fit. He had to stoop and turn sideways to get his shoulders through. I gulped and stood up, but it was like he didn't even see me. "Where'd you get that book?" he demanded.

"What? Oh. On the couch?"

"Give it here. It don't belong to you."

Julie bumped into the room from the kitchen, wiping her hands. "Daddy, it's mine. Mamma left it for me."

He looked like Frankenstein's monster, but without a bolt through his head. Skin stretched over his bones, like a skeleton wrapped in a balloon. But his expression changed when he gazed at Julie. "I don't want you readin' it, Julie," he kind of begged her, like a dog who wants to please his master. "It's trash."

"It is not." She marched toward me and took the book out of my hand. "Daddy, this is Nard. He'll be staying with us. Nard, this is my dad. You can call him 'Farley.'"

"I can?" He scared me. I didn't want to make a mistake.

He looked down on me with a dumb-animal expression and nodded. "Everybody calls me Farley except Julie."

"Go wash up, Daddy." She walked over to him and he bent down so she could kiss him. "You smell."

He did, too.

"Nard?" Julie asked me when he'd gone. "Would you set the table?"

"Sure." My gosh, I thought, as I worked. That monster was Julie's father? What kind of a foster home was this?

Three

I watched a hand wander around on three fingers, looking for something. Its thumb and little finger were like
hands. It could see and hear things, but couldn't talk.

"Better get up, boy."

I jerked awake, afraid somebody would see what I'd
been dreaming about. "What?"

Anna stood by my door wearing exactly what she'd
had on yesterday, without the baseball cap. "Time to get
up," she said. "So's you can catch the bus with Julie and
go to school."

It had started lightening up outside, so I knew it was
after six. I needed to go to the bathroom. Bad. "Okay.
Can—?"

She nodded, reading my mind. "We're all downstairs

havin' some breakfast. You come down when you're ready."

"Nard," Farley said, frowning at me a few minutes later in the kitchen. He sat on one of the chairs around the old wood table in the room. He wore the same clothes too, but smelled better. Julie sat next to him, eating out of a bowl.

Anna had already gone. I heard the tractor rumble outside. Farley got up as I sat down. "'Bye, honey," he said to Julie, bending over and kissing her on the cheek. "You be a good girl."

"'Bye, daddy. Will you be home tonight?"

"No, the railroad has me on that Salt Lake run for ten days." He picked up a lunch pail. "Your back ain't hurtin' today, is it?"

"No daddy. It's fine. I love you."

He lit up like the sun. "That's good." He looked at me. "You take care, boy," he said, kind of like a warning.

"G'bye, sir."

That made him mad. "Don't call me no 'sir,'" he said, angrily. "I'm Farley."

"Okay." I swallowed. "Farley."

Oatmeal for breakfast with sliced peaches on top. Combed honey, fresh milk, and homemade bread. Milk is delicious when it comes right out of a cow. I could have eaten breakfast all day. "Hurry up," Julie said. "We'll miss the bus."

So I had to eat fast, but the tastes stayed in my mouth.

The bus stop was half a mile away. We took a shortcut on a path that skirted the marsh and lake. When the path came to a fence, we ducked through into somebody's pasture. Sleek horses, like postcards I'd seen of thoroughbreds grazing in the fields, were feeding on hay tossed around in piles on the ground. The horses paid no attention to us.

Soon we were on the dirt road that stretched past Anna's farm, south of the lake. When it turned into pavement I saw more great looking lawns and gardens, on both sides of the street. Huge houses hid behind trees with paved lanes leading back to them. It only took ten minutes to walk to the bus stop, but time changed or something. We were back in the world of today.

A couple of kids waited at a corner by a fire hydrant. They chatted away as though we weren't there and even pointed their backs at us. "You'll get used to it," Julie said, aiming her back at them. "The teachers aren't like that except for some I could name. I like the school."

When the bus came, there were only five other kids on it. We sat in the back. "I don't like anyone behind me," Julie said. "I like knowing what they're laughing at."

She had the book Farley was going to kill me for. "How come you like that book so much?" I asked.

"It's about Isadora Duncan, who invented modern dance. I'd like to be her some day."

"Strangled by your own scarf?"

"No! A dancer. An artist. Good at something." She looked out the window. "Women weren't supposed to be like that in 1927, when she died."

"Who cares what women were supposed to be like in 1927?"

"I care," Julie snapped at me. "So did my mom. She ran away to be a dancer, but left this book for me so I'd know why she couldn't take me with her."

I'd wondered a few things about my parents, too. They'd put me in a basket, rung somebody's doorbell, and disappeared. "Where's your mom now?"

"Killed in a car wreck. I used to get postcards from her from all over the world."

"Was she famous?"

"No." Julie frowned and stared hard at something I couldn't see. "But *I* will be, someday."

The way she said it, I believed her.

But a week later, Julie's chances for fame as a dancer took a dive. Her back was so bad she couldn't go to school. She could barely walk.

Four

"Nard, for you!" Julie yelled from her bedroom. "Take it downstairs, okay?"

I'd been reading about famous inventors for a paper I had to write, due the next day in my "History of the World" class. I skipped down the stairs and picked up the telephone. "Hello?"

"Hi Nard," Mrs. Cousins said in her cheerful voice.

"Mrs. Cousins!" It had been a whole month since we'd talked. "I thought you'd forgotten where you put me."

"I wouldn't do that," she said. "How are you doing?"

"Great!" Man, there was a lot I wanted to tell her...but I had to be careful. Julie might be listening in. "I like it here. The school is way better than any in Eldorado. They have accelerated classes. I'm in two, and acing them."

"No complaints?"

"Some," I said. "There's like a war between Anna and everybody else who lives on Bergen Lake. She got here way ahead of any of them, but they want her to move. So there's some trouble."

"Such as?"

"Their kids sneak on the farm and spook the animals and stuff, and the parents won't do anything about it. And the kids at school call me 'Nerd' instead of 'Nard,' but at least they talk to me." The heck with Julie, I decided. If she's listening, maybe it would do her some good. "They won't even talk to Julie."

"They won't? Why not?"

"She's got this chip on her shoulder." I listened for some giveaway sound, but didn't hear any. "All the other kids are rich, and Julie's got this attitude about it. Except there's more to it than that."

"Like what?"

"She's so cool." It surprised me to hear myself talk like that about a girl. But I meant it. "There's something wrong with her back, but you should see her perform when she's strong."

"Perform? What do you mean?"

"She's awesome on gymnastic equipment." I watched her in my mind as we talked, arcing into a routine on the high bar. A small ripple washed through her body, and she swung into a handstand. "When she's on the high bar or the parallel bars or rings, she's way better than anyone else, even the boys. Except she has to rub it in."

"Not the way a girl should be? Is that what you mean?"

"The way anybody should be, Mrs. Cousins. There's this modern dance class, interpretive dancing that she stays for after school? I wait for her so we can ride the bus home together, and she's fantastic." I got excited for some reason, just talking about it. "She does these slow leaps that last minutes instead of a second. Then when we get home she goes out to the barn and practices for hours. No wonder her back kills her." I wiped off my drippy nose, which goes with living on a farm. "But she's always in the teacher's face, like she knows more about it than he does. How can she? She's just a kid."

"You think she should listen more?"

"It sure wouldn't hurt! But her role model is Isadora Duncan, who never listened to anybody." I told her who Isadora Duncan was and how she'd had babies by fathers she wasn't married to, and was a Communist. "Only today, Julie's in bed and can hardly move, and I'm scared."

"What's wrong?"

"Her spine. She might have to go to the hospital. It would kill her if she had to quit dancing."

"Then you have feelings for her?"

"Sure!" I blushed for some reason. "I like everybody, in fact. Even Farley."

"Let's talk about Mrs. Swedenborge first."

"Is this for your report?"

"Yes."

So I told her what a tough old lady Anna was and how hard she worked on the farm, even though there were only sixty-seven acres left. "She smokes a pipe."

"Oh dear," Mrs. Cousins said. "She doesn't encourage you to smoke, does she?"

"No. That old pipe only comes out at night, after all the chores are done and we're sitting on the front porch listening to frogs and crickets. Don't put that in your report, okay?"

"Does she or anyone hit you or abuse you in any way?"

"Anna swats me if I have it coming. But she's the best foster mom I've had, Mrs. Cousins. She hugs me too, just to send a message, like 'You're okay, boy.'"

"What about duties and responsibilities? Are you expected to work for your meals or keep?"

"Could that get her in trouble?"

"Trust me."

"She leaves it up to me, Mrs. Cousins." Then I told her about some of my inventions. "She asked me to feed the pigs and I tried, but it took forever with one hand. So I got Farley to build me a pig feeder. Now everybody uses it."

"What is it?"

"Just an old wagon wheel. I got Farley to hang it from an axle between a couple of posts. We fixed a handle on the rim at the top, and a hook on the rim at the bottom. You hook a bucket of pig slop at the bottom of the wheel, crank it above the fence with the handle, and dump it on the other side into the trough. I figured out a way to get the hens to lay more eggs, too."

"Really. How?"

"The hens are in a hen house. It used to be in the barn, even though they lay better if they're outside in the sun during the day. But the rotten kids throw stuff at them if no one is here. So I put the hen house on a platform with wheels and now we push it in and out of the barn. It's easier to clean, too."

"Then you aren't being stifled, obviously. You're allowed to express your creativity?"

"No problem. Anna says school comes first, and she means it."

"Now tell me about Julie's father," she said. "Everything."

"Why 'everything'?" I asked, suspiciously. "What about him?"

"There's an indication of perhaps a hint of mental instability in his background."

When she talked like that, I knew they'd dug up something bad about Farley. "What's the deal? Was he in the nut house?"

She didn't answer my question right away. "Would that surprise you?"

"Not really. He gets strange sometimes."

"Examples?"

"He thought he could lengthen the TV cable by cutting it and splicing in an extension cord. I thought Anna would kill him."

"Does he hallucinate?"

"You mean like see things that aren't there?" I asked, just to make sure I knew what she meant.

"Yes."

"No."

"Drink?"

"Sometimes, when Anna isn't around. She really lets him know about it if she finds out."

"Does it alter his personality?"

"It turns him into a salesman, sort of. Usually he's quiet and doesn't say much, which works because he doesn't have a lot of brains to work with. But when he drinks, instant expert."

"Nard, promise me something."

"Sure."

"At the slightest indication of harm from Farley Marne, run, okay? Don't try to take anything with you. Just run."

Five

Summer vacation rolled around, which was a relief. I was tired of being called "Nerd." Julie said she hoped all the kids in the neighborhood would go to Europe, because the summer was when they attacked. If they did, at least it wouldn't get boring.

The first Tuesday of the vacation started like a regular day. Farley took the bus into town for work and Anna gave me a list of chores. Then she and Julie drove off in the pickup to the doctor's office. Julie's back hadn't gotten any better, but the doctor thought he knew what the problem was. In layman's language, her spinal column had a kink in it, and the more she grew, the worse it got. He'd taken x-rays and stuff, and that day, Julie was supposed to find out what could be done about it.

I decided the chores could wait. They wouldn't be back for hours, so I took off my shoes and socks and waded into the lake next to the dock.

It was like a nature clinic down there with my feet soaking in muck. Reeds and cattails crowded into the shoreline, water spiders skittered on top of the water, and inch-long insects that looked like flying nails hovered and darted around. The toads in the neighborhood stopped chirping long enough to get used to me and I got interested watching tadpoles squiggle all over—

When someone grabbed me from behind, pinning my arms to my sides! Uh oh, I thought. Rich kids from the other side of the lake? Before I could move, I was wrapped up like an ace bandage, in rope! "Hey!"

"Nard," a faraway voice replied.

It was Farley. He sounded weird. "I thought you took the bus to work."

"I did." He wrapped the rope around me a few more times. "But then I got off the bus and come back." He hoisted me over his shoulder like a sack of flour. "I got an idea."

"You?" I asked. "Got an idea?" I started to laugh... when I remembered what Mrs. Cousins had said. "You'd better put me down, Farley." I angled around his neck to look at his face and got a whiff of his breath. Whiskey.

"I will, Nard," he said, as solemn and deliberate as a judge. "Once we get to the operating room."

"What are you talking about?"

"My Julie needs a backbone that's straight," he told me. "Like yours."

A backbone like mine? Operating room?

"What's more, you're the same age as my Julie," he said, "and practically the same size. I'm gonna open you up and peel your backbone out of you. Same as you do with trout."

"You'll do *what?*"

"Then when Julie's home I plant it in her and sew her up. Before you know it, she'll be as good as new."

"Bone me like a fish?" I thrashed around on his shoulder. But he was three times bigger than me. I wasn't going anywhere. *"With what? A chainsaw?"*

"Nope," he said, calmly. "I'll chisel it out."

A chisel! I could feel him hacking into my back with a chisel, prying out my spine. *"It won't work, man! First you'll kill me, then you'll kill Julie!"*

Then he told me about the voices in his head! The Lord works in mysterious ways, they'd explained to him. He'd put two cripples on Anna's farm for a reason!

"You're crazy!" I screeched at him, squirming around helplessly. *"Put me down!"*

But it was like Farley wasn't there. A robot had charge of his body. "If a sensible man has two busted motors, won't he put them together?" He didn't even sound the same. "For one motor that works is better than two that is broke." He sounded like a preacher reading the Bible! "As it is with motors, so it is with people, for one whole person is better than two cripples."

He hauled me to the barn where Anna keeps the tractor and pushed open the door to the tack room. Then he plopped me on the workbench. It was so dark I couldn't see the dust that stirred up from the dirt floor. But I could taste it. I tried moving, but the only muscles I could use were my vocal chords. "Think about it will you?" I begged him. "A spine isn't a piece of rope!"

"'Course it ain't," Farley said, his voice miles away from his mouth. "I'll have to be very, very careful." Tools hung from a pegboard above the bench. "I won't get no second chance." He grabbed a mallet and a chisel. "It's got to be done right the first time."

"Farley, spines are *complicated*, man!" I screeched at him. "They aren't like zippers!" How could I get through to the crazy? "You can't cut out an old one and put in a new one!" I tried to penetrate his brain with something he could relate to. "Remember when you tried to splice the TV cable? You couldn't even do that!"

"That was a learning experience. Hold still now." He leaned on me with his arms and worked the chisel into the top of my spine just below my hairline. "I don't want to make a mess of things." He picked up the mallet!

I lost it. I wriggled around like a worm on a fishhook. *"You're drunk! Sober up!"* I fell off the workbench and tried rolling away from him on the dirt floor.

"Now look what you done!" he bellowed, dropping on me with his knees. "Hold still, you rotten boy!" He flipped me onto my stomach.

No way could I hold still. Every pore in my back had turned into a howling nerve. "*No!*" I screamed, trying to buck him off... then felt the chisel in the back of my neck. "*NO!*"

With all that bouncing, the chisel knicked the skin. I felt blood, *my* blood, dripping down. He stopped, lowered the mallet, and looked at the end of the chisel. "Izzat blood?"

My mouth had filled with dirt and turned into mud. I was so scared that everything in me shivered, like an icicle plugged into a wall socket. "Yes! *My* blood, you lunatic!"

He jumped off my back and stood up, dropping the tools. "My gosh." He sounded dazed, as though he didn't know where he was. The weirdness slid off his face. "I didn't mean to hurt you none," he said, shaking his head, confused. "You all right boy?" He picked me up carefully, like I was his precious baby.

What I don't get is this. I was grateful to him, and almost said "Thanks!" He set me on the workbench and unwrapped the rope. The robot was gone. The real Farley had come back. "You just come with me, Nard," he said, helping me down. "That neck of yours needs a bandage."

"What the hell gets into you, Farley?" I don't swear much, which you learn after living in a few foster homes.

31

The consequences are too unpredictable. But I was shaking like a leaf and couldn't help myself. "What makes you so crazy?"

"I don't know, boy. Beats me how everything is simple one minute then all mixed up and complicated the next." I didn't have shoes on so he carried me to the back door of the farmhouse. "I get to thinking and maybe that's the problem. Things just seem to close in on me."

"You get to drinking, too."

His eyes squinted at me with pain. "She'll be bent over double before she's sixteen, and I'm her father. She needs my help, Nard. Ain't there anything I can do?"

I should have phoned Mrs. Cousins and told her Farley'd flipped out. But he felt bad enough to kill himself, and I didn't need that on my conscience. So I told him to forget it, instead. He went off to work and I got busy with the chores.

I was feeding pigs when Anna and Julie got back. "Hi!" I yelled, reaching for the handle near the top of the pig-feeder wheel. The truck would be full of supplies. I liked bringing in the groceries and checking them out. "Be there in a sec!" I wound the bucket up, tipped in slop, ducked the splash, then trotted toward the truck.

Something was wrong. Usually Anna bounced out of the cab with more energy than a cyclone, but she was so tired she could barely open the door. Julie sat there too like she couldn't move. "Hey," I said. "Who died?"

"Nobody." Anna's voice dragged along with her feet until she saw the bandage on my neck. "What happened to you, boy?"

"Practicing casts," I told her. "I caught myself with a fishhook."

The pickup had only one sack in it. I picked it up and followed them to the screen porch above the root cellar. They were so quiet I could hear the aspen leaves rattle. "You'd just as well sit a minute, Nard," Anna said, plopping herself in a chair. "There'll be some changes around here and you have a right to know why."

"Auntie, don't change anything," Julie pleaded, leaning on the rickety old table. "Everything has to stay the way it is. Please? It's like this is the only place in the whole world that's real."

It didn't take a rocket scientist to know what the problem was. "What did the doctor say?" I asked Anna.

"Nothin' we couldn't have guessed, I reckon. Julie needs an operation." That didn't sound so terrible, as long as the surgeon wasn't Farley. "The bad part is, it won't wait." Anna stared at the sky like there was something behind it that scared her. "If she don't have it this summer, she could spend the rest of her days in a wheelchair."

"I don't even care," Julie said. "I won't be able to dance anyway."

"Hush, child. Go lay down."

"No. I *hate* lying down all the time."

I didn't get it. "Why is everyone all broken up?" I

asked. "Julie gets operated on and she's okay, right? As soon as she heals up she's back in the gym, training for the Olympics."

"That won't be the way of it," Anna said. "They'll put a rod in her back and doctor says it'll leave her stiff as a flagpole. But at least she'll be able to stand up and walk."

"He also said it would cost fifty thousand dollars," Julie said. "For what? So I can walk around like a scarecrow?"

"Cost?" I asked. "You mean you'd have to pay for it?"

Anna nodded and Julie turned away.

"How come the government won't pay for it? Or what about insurance?" I knew about those things because of my stub. The government won't pay for artificial hands or prosthetic devices for thirteen-year-olds though, and orphans don't have insurance because they aren't anybody's kid. But Julie's case was different, wasn't it?

"You'd think somebody might," Anna said. "But the doctor says it's too 'experimental' or some such. He says it doesn't come in under the government guidelines, and Farley's insurance with the railroad doesn't cover it either."

"What are you going to do?"

"Something I'd'a done long ago if I wasn't so stubborn about things." She put her hands on her knees and pushed down, which levered her up to standing. "Sell the farm."

Six

"Julie?"

She was in her room. The door was closed, but I could hear her crying.

"Go away."

"I brought you a tadpole."

"That's stupid. I don't want a tadpole."

"They're cool, Julie. They have to grow up to find out if they're a toad or a frog."

"They're fish food." The door swung open. "*You* can come in but don't bring it. It's probably dead anyway." She wiped her nose. "Let me see him."

I didn't have one. "Just kidding." I sat on the chair in front of her desk. "You know what I'd like to do this summer?"

"No." She threw herself on her bed, looking like a puppet without the strings that held it up.

"Go to Mars," I told her. "Start a colony." The middle row of her bookcase was jammed with books on ballet and modern dance. A big poster painting of Isadora Duncan, dancing in a meadow, hung on the wall over her bed. "Why don't you come with me?"

"What would I do on Mars?" She plopped a pillow against the wall and leaned on it. "I know. The clown act."

"No. Tend the generators. Create the atmosphere. Plant the wheat. Like that."

"Boring. I thought you were going to talk about sex."

"Sex!"

"You said start a colony, Nard. What am I supposed to think?" She glared at me, like I'd done something wrong. "Don't look at me like it never crossed your mind. How else would you start a colony? Besides, you're a guy." She fluffed the pillow. "That's all guys ever think about."

"I wasn't thinking about that," I said. "I meant help me get the place ready for the settlers and pioneers who'd follow."

"I can't go. I've got my own agenda this summer."

"What?"

"I'm going to give myself a big party, then kill myself."

"Come off it, Julie. Where's the fun in that?"

"There isn't any fun in living either." Her eyes were still red and she wiped her nose with her hand. "I mean it *could* be fun if I could dance." Slowly, in a way I can't even explain, her body rolled into a ball. Then her feet lifted through the air, pulling the rest of her along in a smooth arc. She landed on the floor on her feet. But her face tightened with pain and she fell back on the bed. "It won't happen," she said, finding her pillow and giving it a hug. "I'll be an old witch, Nard. An ugly old witch."

She didn't need to feel sorry for herself. I'd tried that and it doesn't work. "So?" I asked her. "You'd fit on a broom."

"That's not very nice."

"Being a witch might not be as bad as you think," I said. "Witches can fly. We could meet on Mars."

She sat up and rubbed her nose on her knees. "Do you ever think about what you want out of life?"

"Sure." I leaned back in the chair and propped my feet on her desk. "Money. Piles of it. Tons of it."

"Really?" She sounded surprised. "I mean, you're so cool. You're the last person I thought would care about money. I thought with you it was just, you know, laugh and be happy."

"Show me an orphan and I'll show you someone who wants to be a millionaire," I told her. "Orphans are poor. Most of them drop out of high school for really great jobs, like in a fast food restaurant."

"What would you do if you had money?"

"All kinds of stuff." I visualized myself surrounded by electronic toys. "I'd buy the best PC there is, and the fastest modem, and hook into the Internet and write my own programs and draw pictures and play war games. I'd buy houses all over the world, like in Switzerland and South Africa and a mansion in Maine next to Stephen King. I'd fly around in a Learjet."

"Would you get a hand?"

"They're called 'prosthetic devices' and I'd fill up a closet with them. One for playing an electric guitar, one to eat with, one to drive my cool Beemer with, one to swat mosquitoes. I'd get your back fixed, too."

"You would?"

I nodded. "Before your old man kills both of us."

"What are you talking about?"

I told her how he'd almost operated on me.

Instantly, she felt better! "I didn't think he even *knew*," she said, as though she'd made a huge discovery. "He never says anything to *me*."

"Sure he does. You just don't hear him."

She didn't hear me either. Her head rocked back and forth and she smiled. "He must love me, to do something *that* crazy." Right, I thought. If Mrs. Cousins knew what he'd done, the slug would be in jail. "Did you know your parents, Nard?"

"No. They left me in a basket and ran off."

"Farley's kind of weird now, but he was great until my mom went off to be a dancer. I mean *I* thought he was nice. My poor mom couldn't stand him."

"Why am I not surprised?"

"Do you like it here?" She cradled her face in her hands and stared at me. "I mean on the farm with Anna and Farley?"

"It's okay."

"She's thinking about selling the farm! Can you believe it? The developers would fall all over each other to buy it, but she can't stand people like that."

"Why? If somebody wanted to give me a bunch of money, I'd probably like them."

"Because they ruin everything. You've heard Anna talk about how nice it was out here when she was a girl?"

"Maybe taking care of you means more to her than a bunch of old memories."

"That stupid operation won't do any good. The doctor won't even guarantee it. He told us even if it works, I'll be a physically challenged freak." She twisted around and stood up, but the tumbling move had done something bad. When she tried to walk, she had to push her hands down on her hips like an old person. "Auntie's lived here all her life. She remembers how it used to be, practically when the Indians hunted buffalo."

"Or Buffalo Bill." I aimed down my stub like it was a rifle and pulled the trigger. "Blam!" My arm kicked up. "Got him!"

"Promise me something, Nard?"

"What?" I said, blowing smoke out of the barrel.

"If something happens to me you'll stay with Aunt Anna?"

"What are you talking about?" I forgot all about the buffalo I'd shot. "Nothing's going to happen to you."

"Just promise me, okay?"

"No! Then you'll think it's okay to kill yourself."

"Tell me why I shouldn't." She pushed her hips with her hands but her back wouldn't straighten out. "I'm like a drain on society. It hurts to *move* and I *love* movement!" Then she sat down on the bed, carefully, like there were eggs under the mattress that she didn't want to break. "I'm a weed. I should be pulled up by the roots and tossed out."

"Don't talk like that. Even if you could have been the greatest dancer in the universe, it's not okay to kill yourself. Okay?" It surprised me that I talked like that. What difference did it make to me?

"Why not?"

"Because you've got a family. A dad, anyway. So you could have done better in that department. Still, you've got one. And an aunt. And me too, kind of."

"*You* aren't in my family. We're not related."

I got up so fast the chair I'd been sitting on crashed to the floor. Rule Number One when you're an orphan is don't ever think you're in somebody's family. "I sure don't know why I said *that*," I shouted, running for the door. I stopped and stared at her from the hall. "You want to kill yourself? Be my guest!"

Seven

Julie and I quit talking, Anna had her brain full of all kinds of stuff, and Farley never said anything anyway. It got very quiet around there for the next few days. I still heard Anna in the early morning when she fed the animals, but her heart wasn't in it. Instead of talking to them the same way she did to people who were good friends, feeding them became a chore she could hardly wait to finish.

The next Wednesday afternoon, after what would have been a full day's work for anyone else, she and Julie dressed to go to town. Farley had already taken the bus to work. "Will you be all right, boy?" Anna asked when she and Julie were in the truck. "You don't mind us runnin' out on you this way?"

"I don't mind." I avoided looking at Julie. "There's lots

to do. I'll mend that fence by the holding pen where it was cut."

"Don't see how you'll do that with only one hand," Anna said, "but you're good at riggin' things. You just might come up with a brand new invention. Isn't that so, Julie?"

Julie didn't say anything. She just stared in front of her as though she hadn't heard.

"Stop it you two!" Anna said, all of a sudden. It blew out of her like a geyser out of the ground. "I'm gonna feed both of you weed poison if you don't patch things up! It's hard enough without you two actin' like congressmen!" She started the truck and jammed it in gear, then took some deep breaths to cool down. "We'll be back by supper," she said to me. "You keep a sharp eye out while we're gone, hear? That fence didn't cut itself. Why don't those boys get jobs and leave us alone?"

"Work?" I said, at exactly the same time Julie said, "Jobs?" It was kind of funny and we looked at each other and laughed.

"G'bye, Nard," Julie said. "I'm sorry."

"I'm the one who should apologize," I said.

"That's better," Anna said. "That's one good thing for today."

As soon as they were gone I headed for the kitchen, rather than the fence. Anna had baked some bread and the smells were driving me crazy. I took a fresh loaf from the pantry, hacked off a big chunk and dunked it in homemade applesauce. I ate the whole loaf, then drank a quart of fresh milk.

I was so stuffed I could barely move.

There was no use trying to mend fence. I waddled out to the screen porch and stretched on the couch that makes into a bed. A magazine of Julie's was there and I picked it up, propped a pillow under my head, and started to read an article about street theater. It had pictures of a guy riding a unicycle through an inner city obstacle course. They showed him hopping up steps and curbings, then weaving through boxes and garbage pails.

But I couldn't concentrate. My head drooped down and jerked back up. Nap time, I decided...when I heard a noise by the screen door. It sounded like the scratch a dog makes when it wants someone to let it in.

I looked in that direction and saw a Hand. It didn't surprise me. The magazine collapsed on my stomach and I relaxed, watching the hand try to squeeze under the door.

Parts of the house had settled in the ground. In places you could roll marbles down the floor. A big gap yawned between the bottom of the screen and the wooden deck near the door jamb. I watched the thing search patiently for the best place to crawl, like a spider trying to climb out of a bath tub...when with a quick move, it rolled onto the porch!

I sat up. What a great dream I thought, watching it get its bearings. It stood up on three fingers and walked toward me.

"Hold it," I said.

Don't get excited, I told myself. Just an unattached hand. A left hand too, which I could use, like the one in my dreams. The definition was better, though. It had long thin fingers, like a concert pianist. It stopped four feet from the couch and seemed to look up at me.

I laughed. This was the coolest dream I'd ever had. "Hi," I said. "Can you talk?"

It shook kind of like its head "no" and did pantomime.

"Paper?" I asked. "You want a piece of paper?"

It jumped up twice and touched the tips of its fingers like a tap dancer clicking its heels. An obvious "yes."

"Wait a sec," I said, jumping off the couch. I edged around the quirky little thing, keeping a comfortable distance, to an old desk next to the wall. I opened the drawer, found a piece of paper, and put it on the floor.

The Hand picked the paper up between its thumb and index finger. It marched on two fingers to the magazine on the floor next to the couch, and spread the sheet on the magazine. Then it did some more pantomime, this time like holding a pencil.

"Gotcha."

I found a pencil in the kitchen. In the distance I heard a siren and wondered what a siren was doing in my dream. I ran back to the porch and handed it the pencil.

It was different from the hands I'd dreamed about. It was an old hand, like Anna's, with age splotches on it, but bigger and stronger than hers. It was a man's hand.

He held the pencil like a chopstick, and started writing.

Something was radically wrong with the way he wrote. He started on the right side of the page and moved left, spilling letters along the line like out of a can of alphabet soup.

"Praise be to God. At last, I have found you."

"I can't read that," I told him.

He grabbed a corner of the paper between his thumb and little finger. Dragging the paper along behind like a tail, he strolled into the house. He took long strides on his three middle fingers and zipped along without seeming to hurry. He knew exactly where to go. The bathroom. Then like a monkey he swung up the pipes under the sink, somehow looping into the wash basin while holding on to the sheet of paper. He aimed the paper at the mirror over the sink.

I saw the reflection. "Praise be to God," the words said. It had been written backwards! "At last, I have found you."

"Cool!"

But the volume on the siren turned up. It started vibrating like an earthquake in progress . . . when two police cars roared into the back yard! Suddenly the sound stopped, so fast it left echoes hanging in stillness. Then a voice thundered over a loudspeaker. "Leonard Smith, we know you're in there!" it boomed. "Come out! This is the Sheriff of Bergen County! Come out immediately, with your hands in the air!"

Eight

What did the cops want with me? I hadn't done anything wrong! I ran into the living room and peeked through the curtains of the window. A police car with lights flashing stood right in the middle of the lawn! Two officers crouched behind it with rifles, aimed at the house!

"Come out immediately, Leonard Smith!" the voice roared. "You have thirty seconds. One. Two. Three..."

I turned to ice. Would they really shoot me? I needed a hiding place and turned around to look for one when my foot caught on something and I smacked into the floor.

The Hand. But that had been a dream, hadn't it? He skittered under the couch, out of sight.

The cop cars in the yard were not a dream. Could I sneak out the back? I ran for the screen porch. But a patrol car guarded the back yard! Two sheriff's hats and two gun barrels pointed at me from behind it! "... Sixteen. Seventeen..."

I thought of crazy things like calling for help. Maybe if I dialed 911?

The counting stopped! "Leonard Smith, you are surrounded," blasted the voice. "Come out of the residence immediately. Do not, repeat, do not harm the girl! Give yourself up!"

What girl? Julie?

She was at the doctor's! All I had to do was explain. Right?

Right. I was so scared I couldn't feel my feet. I floated to the front of the house, took a deep breath, shut my eyes, and opened the door. My right hand and left stub stuck in the air like antlers, and I stood there. It felt like standing in front of a firing squad.

"Move forward, sir. Slowly."

I opened my eyes enough to see, and crept across the front porch one step at a time. A whole army of cops hid behind the patrol car with guns aimed right at my stomach. A bronze shield on the door of the patrol car said, "To serve and protect."

I stumbled down the steps, into bright sunlight. The officer with the big horn in his hand spoke up again. "Stop." He didn't need the microphone. He was only twenty feet away. "What have you done with the girl?"

"Nothing."

"Who else is in the house?"

"Nobody." Then I remembered the Hand. Should I tell them about him? No way! They didn't need to think I was crazy, too.

I saw Farley! There he was, staring at me through the back window of a patrol car! The window was up and the glass had a tint, but Farley's old face peeked through like a statue carved out of rock.

A woman officer stood up and motioned me forward. "Move over here, Leonard," she said. "By the car." I did. "You can put your hands down." I lowered my hand and stub. "Lean against the car on your elbows."

"Okay," I said.

Three huge guys came out from behind the patrol car with their guns aimed at me. She ran her hands over my body. "He's clean," she said. "He's scared, too."

"Fear can make them twice as dangerous," the cop with the horn said. He opened the door of the patrol car, pointed at Farley, and asked me, "Do you know this man?"

"Yes sir." Farley sat in the back seat with his hands behind him. Handcuffed?

"What's his name?"

"Farley Marne."

"How do you know him?"

I gulped, wondering what this was all about. "He lives here. I do, too."

"Who is Anna Swedenborge?"

"She's his aunt. She owns the farm."

Another officer spoke up. "Hey kid, you don't mind if we go in there and look around, do you?"

"No."

"Wha'di'ya think, Sarge?"

The officer with the horn looked at me through slits, then stuck his head into the car. "Dispatch, do you copy?"

"Copy," a voice said. It sounded like over the telephone, but came from somewhere inside the car.

"Take Dornan and Halloran," the cop with the horn said. "Proceed with extreme caution. This could be our gang."

"Those burglaries you mean? Out in Bergen Heights?"

"Exactly," Sarge said. "This farm would make a great hideout. They've got to be locals, know the territory."

The officer stared at the house with determination. "Halloran, get Dornan," he said to the woman. "He's with the unit in back. I'm goin' in." He ran in a low crouch for the front porch, holding his rifle like a commando. I watched him kick the door open and jump inside.

"A gang of burglars?" I asked the sergeant.

The big cop acted like he hadn't heard me. "Get in the car, young man." He held the front door on the passenger side for me. I climbed in. He reached across me and clipped a handcuff to the steering wheel. "Let me have your hand," he said. I held up the only one I have. He clipped the other end of the handcuff to it, then shut the door and motioned to the other officers. They walked toward the house.

I waited until they were far enough away so they couldn't hear us. "What's going on, Farley?"

"I can't do anything right," he said, miserably. "I can't even hold up a bank right."

"What?"

"I got to get money, Nard. For Julie."

"You robbed a bank?"

"It come to me all at once," he said. "This great idea."

His eyes were bloodshot, the way they get when he drinks. "So you didn't go to work this morning?" I asked him. "You went to a liquor store instead?"

"How'd you know that?"

"That's when you get your great ideas. What bank?"

"That little tiny bank in that shopping center near where you and Julie go to school."

"What happened?"

"I had it all worked out in my mind," he said. "It almost worked too."

"I'll bet."

"Well, it did." He sounded proud of himself. "The first thing, I got me the realest-looking toy gun there is. I bought it at a toy store where I get off the bus in Eldorado. Then I marched into the jewelry store right next door and stuck that gun in the clerk's face. I give him the sack from the toy store and told him to fill it up with money and jewels, if he knew what was good for him." He sounded smug about it. "He opened up the cash register and stuffed money in there, then scooped up some jewels and put them in too, and I ran out of there with the sack. It was easy, just like I knew it would be!"

"But you got caught. Right?"

"Nope. I got outside and there was a cab just waiting for me. I said to the driver, take me out to Bergen Lake. I was comin' home with the money! But when I looked inside that sack there wasn't hardly enough in there for cab fare. That's when I had him stop at that bank."

"Uh oh."

"There was people in it and a guard. But I had experience by this time and figured out a plan. There was a woman teller and a man teller so I went to the woman, thinking she'd be easier to rob. When the guard turned around I sidled up to her and stuck that gun on the counter and looked her right in the eye, but you know what she done? She punched the alarm!" He sighed. "I tried to walk out, but the guard, he come over and arrested me in front of everybody."

"Then what happened?"

"They took me to the sheriff's office and told me I had a right to a lawyer. But I knew that'd make things worse." He got kind of fidgety. "That's when I got this other idea."

"Another idea?"

He looked at his feet. "You won't mind, will you, boy? I can't go to jail, you see that, don't you? I got to get money for Julie."

"What was your idea?"

"I made up a story. I told them you'd kidnapped her and was holdin' her for ransom, thinking they'd let me go. Instead they made me tell them where you had her tied up, and it didn't work out right."

"Is that why they came out here looking for me?"

"It's nice in that jail, Nard. The food ain't much but it's clean and there's TV and it's warm. They'd be satisfied with just one criminal, be my guess. Then I can figure out some way to—"

"You want me to take the blame? You think if I do that, you won't have to go to jail?"

"It ain't like you got a family. You'll do it, won't you, boy? For Julie?"

It didn't take long for me to make up my mind. "No!"

A few minutes later, I thought I'd be going to jail anyway. The big cop with the bullhorn wanted to take me in! "Why?" I asked him. "I didn't do anything. Someone has to stay here and feed the pigs."

We went into the house and called my caseworker. "Do you want me to bring him in?" he asked Mrs. Cousins, after telling her what had happened. Then he handed me the telephone.

"What is going on, young man?" She sounded excited.

"It's really complicated," I told her. "Julie's at the doctor with Anna. She needs an operation, but they don't have the money to pay for it. They need me, Mrs. Cousins. Especially if Farley goes to jail."

"I'm thinking of you. Did that man do anything to you?"

I had to shut my eyes. "No."

"Are you telling me the truth?"

"Yes."

"He'll be out of jail in a day or two, Nard. How dangerous is he?"

"He does dumb things, but wouldn't hurt anybody. He's just a father."

"Are you telling me the truth?" she asked, again.

"I wouldn't lie to you, Mrs. Cousins."

"All right. Let me talk to the officer."

She told him she was "encouraged by my sense of responsibility," and it would be in "my best interest" to stay.

What a relief, I thought, when they finally drove away. But the smile on my face didn't last very long. Maybe two seconds.

Nine

When the patrol cars drove off, they dragged a big dust cloud behind them until they got to the paved road. I was still watching when I heard a noise behind me and turned around.

Three high school guys who lived on the other side of the lake crawled out of the root cellar! "What a bunch of grunge," Erik Robinson said in a man's voice. He was the only one whose name I knew. "Those stupid bleeps! I didn't think they'd leave, man." He laughed and brushed stuff off his blue jeans.

"Hey, we've got their attention!" the guy with dark hair said. His voice had changed, too. "Did you hear the pig? We've got like a name. Bergen Heights Burglars!" He laughed. "Hey bleephead," he said to me. "Aren't you gonna invite us in?"

"No." Was this the gang the police were after? "You guys leave. You shouldn't..."

Erik pulled out a gun and pointed it at me! It wasn't a toy, either. "Listen, Nard or whatever your name is. We're going to look around. Do you have a problem with that?"

"No sir," I said.

"That's better." He stuck the gun in a holster over his back pocket. "Come on," he said to the others and walked toward the house.

"Are you just gonna let him go?" the guy with black hair asked. "What if he fingers us to the cops?"

"He won't say anything, Mikey," Erik said. "Not if he wants to go on living. Who'd believe him anyway? It'd be our word against his."

"You know something?" the other boy said. "My dad told me they're so poor they cook off an old wood stove." They laughed and walked into the house as if they owned it.

I heard them in there, laughing and talking and dumping things on the floor. "Look at this, Fish! Can you believe this?" I snuck up to the window and watched. Mikey had Anna's old manual typewriter in his hands. "Out of the last century." He dropped it. "See if it breaks."

"There's nothin' here worth stealing," Fish said. "This stuff I wouldn't put out at a garage sale." I heard a crash. "Lookit that old TV, Erik. Rabbit ears!"

They stopped. "What was that?" Erik asked.

"I don't know," Mikey said. "Is that kid up to something cute?"

Quiet again. "Hey! Grab it!" BOOM! The gun went off! "I hit it!" Erik said. "What?" Fish said. "A sheet? It's still floatin'!" BOOM! "Look out!" A crash, followed by another one. "I'm out'a here," Fish said. "Me too," added Mikey. "This place is trapped!" Erik said. They ran out onto the front porch. "Don't they know traps are illegal?" "Where's that kid?"

I heard Anna, driving in on the dirt road.

"You." Erik pointed the pistol at me from the porch. "We weren't here. You got that? The cops wrecked the place when they searched it."

That made me mad. "Anna! Julie!" I yelled, ducking behind the house and running for the truck. "Get the police!" I rounded the corner of the house just as they were climbing out. Anna stood next to the truck in her old dress like a pioneer woman. "Erik has a gun!"

"What?" Anna asked.

"Erik! Mikey! Fish! From the other side of the lake!"

"Here? Now?"

"Yes!"

She grabbed a rake that was propped against the screen porch and ran into the house. Julie and I followed along behind.

They were gone, but the inside of the house was a mess. "Will you look at this," Anna said. "They've never done *this* before."

"I don't see anyone," Julie said. "Where did they go?"

"They ran out the front," I said. "They were just here!"

"Are you sure, boy?" Anna asked me.

My gosh. Didn't she believe me? "Yes!" I heard a motorboat and ran to the porch that faces the lake. A sleek looking speedboat curved away from Anna's dock. "There!"

Anna and Julie came out to the porch, too. But they were too late. There was a boat on the other side of the lake, but it was too far away to see who was in it.

Anna and Julie didn't know what to think. When I told them Farley'd been arrested for robbing a bank, Anna wanted me to tell it to her again. "Call the Sheriff if you don't believe me," I said.

She did, then she ran for the door. "That man has the brain of a turnip!"

"What about this mess?" I asked, kind of miffed. "They even shot up the house! Shouldn't we call the sheriff?"

"Did you say one of those boys was Erik Robinson?" Anna asked, worried about something.

"Yes! He had the gun!"

"Don't call the sheriff just now, boy," she said. "I'll explain later. You children will just have to clean up the best way you can." She tore out of there in a cloud of dust.

"Are you sure my dad robbed a bank?" Julie asked, in a daze.

"No. He just tried." I started picking things off the floor in the living room.

Julie worked too, but her mind was out in space. We stood the furniture in the living room back up and picked up what had been dumped on the floor. After that I took the kitchen and Julie the bathroom. "The window's broken," she said. "Why would they do that?" Then she came to me with a piece of paper in her hand. "What's this?" She showed it to me.

"Praise be to God. At last, I have found you."

"You won't believe this," I said. "A Hand did that. He writes backwards."

She tilted her head at me. "Who are you kidding?"

"Nobody. Look at it in the mirror."

Instead, she wadded it up and threw it at me. "I don't believe anything you've said!" she said, angrily. "My dad isn't in jail. He isn't *that* stupid. What really happened while we were gone?"

"Julie, I didn't do this!" I said, pointing at the mess. "There are bullet holes around here too. My gosh."

"Show me the holes."

"*I* don't know where they are. There are two of them."

"Right."

It wasn't the first time someone thought I'd lied about something I hadn't lied about. When you live in other people's homes, it goes with the territory. I hate it. Julie watched cartoons on television, ignoring me, but the message was clear. You made the mess, you clean it up. I looked all over for bullet holes... the bathroom window! "Julie! In here!"

I showed her how the glass had splintered in long shards, like rays from the sun. Some of the shards had a little piece gouged out at the tip. There was also a small hole in the screen, like someone had punched a pencil through. "If we put these pieces of glass together like a puzzle, we'd see the hole."

She wasn't convinced. But at five o'clock the news came on.

Farley's stupid grin filled the screen. "A Bergen County man is in jail this evening for two robberies," the voice of the anchorperson announced. The image faded to the studio and the screen showed Polly Chan behind a desk. The weatherman grinned at the camera from one side of her and the sports commentator beamed at it from her other side. "Channel Nine believes he's the world's unluckiest robber. That story, and the rest of the news, after these messages."

"*Two* robberies?" Julie asked, staring blankly at the tube. She didn't move during the commercial. "Where did they get that awful picture?" It didn't look bad to me. At least his hair was combed.

The news team returned. Polly Chan told how Farley Marne, from Bergen County, tried to rob the bank at the Sun City Shopping Center with a toy pistol. Unfortunately for Mr. Marne, the teller realized the weapon was a toy when she saw a bar-coded price tag taped to the bottom of the grip.

"Surprise, surprise," the weatherman said.

"That was just the beginning of Mr. Marne's incredible string of bad luck," said Polly Chan.

The security guard at the bank, using a real gun, put Marne under arrest and held him for the Bergen County Sheriff. "He admitted the robbery, but said he had to, to save his daughter. She'd been kidnapped by a drug-crazed boy." She smiled, letting TV-land in on the joke. "He claimed if he didn't get thousands of dollars, the boy would kill his daughter."

"He told them you were going to kill me?" Julie asked.

"Farley and his great ideas," I said.

"The Bergen County investigators didn't believe him," Polly Chan said. "But they have to take those things seriously. Like bomb threats in buildings, they can't take chances." Three cars filled with armed deputies swarmed through the "peaceful Bergen County countryside for a farm on Bergen Lake." They found a boy living there who knew Mr. Marne, but he wasn't drug-crazed and there was no girl. There was no indication of criminal activity.

Julie's hand covered her mouth. "I could die," she said. "I'm sorry for what I said, Nard."

"That's okay."

She wouldn't let herself cry. "Do they have to laugh at him?"

Up to that point, no one had connected Mr. Marne with an earlier robbery of a jewelry store, Polly Chan told everyone in the state. But the deputies left him in a patrol car with the young man. Mr. Marne talked about the other robbery to the boy. What he didn't know was that the radio in the car had been left on. "They recorded his confession to the other robbery!" she said, laughing. "Making him the world's unluckiest robber."

The news team on Channel Nine really got off on it. Julie hid her face in her hands, as though the whole world was laughing at her. They ended the story by reporting that if Farley got convicted of both robberies, he could go to prison for forty years. "Two for the price of one."

Julie, who never cries, cried. "He can't stand being locked up," she said. "It's like he has claustrophobia. He'll die."

Ten

Anna stormed into the kitchen two hours later, just as the sun dropped behind the mountains. Her jaw stuck out and her eyes were on fire. "That father of yours is more trouble than he is worth," she said to Julie. "Are you all right, child?"

"I guess." Julie'd been wandering around like a lost person, rubbing her eyes. After the newscast, the telephone had been ringing a lot. Julie would answer it, listen a couple of seconds, then slam it down. "What will they do to Daddy?"

"Don't worry about him." Anna sounded disgusted and sat down at the table. "He'll stay in jail tonight, which won't hurt him none. The lawyer will get him out tomorrow."

"You hired a lawyer?" Julie asked. "Doesn't that take money?"

"They don't come cheap. I'll get the money from Mr. Robinson in the morning. The lawyer says as soon as she has it, she'll get Farley out of jail."

Robinson! "Erik Robinson's old man?"

"I don't like that man at all, or his son, neither." Her jaw got tighter. "It rankles me to have to deal with him. Sit down, children. I'll tell you what's goin' on."

There were a lot of reasons Anna didn't like Mr. Robinson, we found out. He lived in that big house across the lake with lights on that kept her awake at night, and his son was mean and out of control. "But he's a banker," she told us, "and knows how much this old farm is worth." A week ago, she'd gone to him about a loan to pay for Julie's back operation. Before he would lend her the money, she'd have to mortgage the farm to his bank. "Then if I don't make the payments on time, the bank gets the farm."

"Auntie, did you?" Julie asked.

"No, child. It's just something I was thinking over."

But the thing with Farley changed things, she went on. The lawyer she found had to have twenty thousand dollars right away. Ten thousand would be her fee, and the other ten would be deposited with the court before they'd let Farley out of jail. So she went back to Robinson to see if he'd lend her the money, "and he said he'd have it for me tomorrow, and I won't have to pay him back until October. But there's a condition." Her mouth chewed away, but there was nothing in there to chew on. "If I can't pay him back on time, I have to sell him the farm."

I tried to look on the bright side. At least I'd have a place to live until October.

"Nard," Anna said, glaring at me, "tell me what those boys done when they was here."

I did, how they'd crawled out of the root cellar right after the sheriff drove away and laughed about something the police had said. Erik had a gun and pointed it at me and made threats, then they went into the house and trashed it, but something scared them. Erik shot at it twice.

"What scared them?"

How could I tell her it might have been an unattached Hand? "I don't know," I said. "Mice?"

She shook her head, but let it go. "What did the police say that they laughed at?"

"They'd gotten their attention?" I asked myself, out loud. "Bergen Heights Burglars or something like that."

"You don't say!" She got up. "Well, that's something. Have you children had your dinner?"

"Not exactly," I said. "But I'm full." I'd had two tomatoes, half a pound of cheese, and a quart of milk.

"I'm not hungry," Julie said.

"Then let's go to work. Nard, I'll need help feedin' the

animals. And Julie, there's the laundry to do. The kitchen floor could use a scrub too, and we're clear out of bread."

"I just want to cry, Auntie."

"Cry then. It won't help none." She glared, like at herself. "But don't let that stop you. It might do *you* some good."

"What will happen to you, Auntie? Where will you live?"

"Us, child. Come over here."

Anna wrapped Julie in her arms. "When you're done with your cry, I want you to put your hands to work."

"Why? What's the use?"

Anna patted her on the back. "The Lord takes better care of them as takes care of themselves, is what the use is." She kissed Julie on top of the head. "When our luck changes, and it will because that's the way of it with luck, what good will it do if we've given up?"

Anna wore me out. We gathered eggs from the hen house, fed those smelly pigs, put a patch over some fence, turned the sheep into a small pasture, and put out water and salt. We tried picking apples and tomatoes by moonlight, but it didn't work. We dragged ourselves into the house at ten o'clock.

Julie had an apron on. Her hair had been tied in a bandana, and the smells from the kitchen were good enough to pull people off the streets. She'd baked bread, apple pie, and made a stew that simmered in the crock pot. The floor was clean enough to eat on, and clothes were hanging on the line outside.

Anna beamed a big smile at her. "Now that's the way!" she said, giving Julie a hug. Then she motioned me over and wrapped me up in her skinny old arms, too. It felt good in there, after all that had happened that day. "I'm proud of you children," she said. "Mighty proud. Let's just see if Julie's cooking tastes as good as it smells!"

It did. I ate a ton, then went to bed. I could hardly wait to crawl under the covers, and snapped off the lamp on my desk. The moon hung over Bergen Peak. I got in bed and watched it through the window, letting my eyes close…when I saw the Hand again! He climbed on my desk and turned the lamp back on.

I sat up and watched him drape himself over the edge of the table. He reached for the knob of the drawer, yanked it open, and fell inside. After mucking around in there he found paper and a pencil, got up on the table, and started writing.

Definitely not a dream. I got out of bed, went over to the table, and watched as he wrote backwards. I translated the turned-around letters into words as soon as they spilled onto the page. "My young Master, the time has come for us to converse. As I have the wit to understand your speech, so are you able to read my written replies. Shall we begin?"

"Begin what?"

"Your instruction, young Leonardo. I have waited patiently through the centuries for your return."

"Waited for me?" I didn't need that! Did that old hand have an agenda for me? "You've got the wrong guy," I told him. "I'm not 'Leonardo.'"

"Surely you have wondered from whence came your name?"

"What's to wonder about? Smith is a popular name for orphans."

"What of Leonard?"

"So? Some idiot at the Department of Social Services tagged me with Leonard. Big deal."

"Could it not be that you are the descendant of a man named Leonardo?" it wrote in that backwards way.

"Anything's possible."

"And is it not possible that this Leonardo was from a village in Italy known as 'Vinci'?"

"As in Leonardo da Vinci?" I shook my head "no." "That definitely would not be my first guess."

"My young Master, you are much, much more than the descendant of Leonardo da Vinci. You are his reincarnation. I bow to you." It stopped writing long enough to do a little bow. "As Kings bowed to the previous Master, I bend to you in honor of your greatness, and out of respect."

This was crazy. No one bowed to me unless they wanted to make fun of me. "I'm going back to bed."

"Nard?" Anna called at me through the door. "Aren't you in bed yet?"

I jumped in. "Yes."

"Your light's still on," she said. "I can see the light under your door. You want me to come in there and turn it off?"

The Hand snapped it off, then hid. "Never mind," I said.

"Now how did you do that, boy?" She opened the door and saw that I was in bed.

I didn't say anything. I was too tired.

"Well, it don't surprise me," Anna said, shutting the door. "I wonder if that boy don't have too many brains."

$\mathcal{E}$leven

I staggered out of bed. It was broad daylight outside and I should have been up hours ago. Anna had let me sleep in.

A piece of paper lay on my desk and I thought Anna had left me a note. I stumbled over there and picked it up.

"'˙sǝlɔɐɹᴉɯ ʞɹoʍ oʇ ɥsᴉʍ I'"

What the heck was that?

Then I remembered the Hand. I read the line from the other direction:

"'I wish to work miracles!'"

The weird stuff from yesterday instantly exploded in my brain. The next line said, "'Do not those words resonate in your soul?'"

They did not "resonate" in my soul. I didn't know what "resonate" meant. I grabbed my dictionary and looked it up: "to resound." *That* helped a lot. It took some chasing around from one definition to the next to get the idea. It meant set off vibes, or something.

I listened for vibes.

Nothing. What resonated with me was money, not miracles. I read the rest of his note.

"'Those are your words, young Master, written 500 years ago.'" My words? I wouldn't write something as dumb as that! "'If history repeats, you will live in great poverty, for that seems always to be the fate of those who would stir dead water into life.'" Live in great poverty? That's what I'd always lived in, and it sucks! "'Your reward, though not capable of measurement in the vulgar manner of the ordinary man, will far exceed in its richness the blatant ugliness and posturing which presently consumes the petty minds of the masses.'"

What a jerk. He wanted to pump me up to work for nothing! I felt a tug on my pajamas.

"Yikes!" He was on the floor, looking up at me. Like a huge insect, he swarmed up the table leg and marched to the middle of the flat surface.

Ideas started firing in my brain. Here was opportunity, glaring me in the face. "Hi," I said, smiling at him. "What's your name?" I handed him a sheet of paper and a pencil and waited, but he looked like he didn't understand me. "You know. What am I supposed to call you?"

"Whatever you wish," he wrote. "For I am at your service, young Master."

I could call him Creep. Or Quirk. But he was too old for names like that. "I wish for you to tell me what name you want."

It took him a while. Then he wrote, "Vinci."

I could live with that. "Okay, Vinny," I said, like we were pals. "I read..."

He jumped up and down, letting me know something was wrong. "No no no," he wrote. "Vinci."

Some people are particular about how you say their name. I guess the same thing goes for unattached hands. "'Vinci'?" I asked him, giving it my best Italian accent. He stood there, glaring in a way. I could tell he wasn't satisfied. "'Vinci,'" I said. "'Vinci.'" Then I tried real hard, stressing the first part and giving the *ci* sound kind of a *she* twist. "'Vinci.'"

"Si!" he wrote. "Yes. You may call me Vinci."

"Okay. I read your note, Vinci," I told him. "You want to do miracles, right?"

"Not I, young Leonardo. You. My wish is to assist, for that is the limit of my power."

"You're like my left hand, the one I wasn't born with?"

"Precisely. With my aid, you will achieve the miracles you set out to accomplish centuries ago! And not a moment too soon, for the earth has become a cesspool. Yet you have the facility, through imagination and intellect, to effect most glorious change. Your mission is to transform Madam Earth into a Garden of Eden. She desperately wishes to regain her true beauty but cannot, because of the ignorance of Mankind."

"So it's like get her a new dress or something?"

"A most apt metaphor! You are indeed The Master!"

Right. "What it takes is money," I said to him. "Ever do tricks?"

"I fail to see the relevance of your question."

"If we had money we could buy her a new dress. Let's make money! I'll show you some tricks and we'll team up and do guest appearances, like on David Letterman, or Jay Leno."

"Money may be needed to acquire those materials with which to conduct experiments," he wrote, kind of sneering at me, "but the pursuit of money is not a worthy goal. The Creator of All Things has endowed you with a superb mind. You have the ability to understand Nature in all her power and magnificence. He has blessed you with the ability to magnify the beauty of Nature, rather than consume her in huge, gluttonous gulps. You must realize the miracles you envisioned 500 years ago. Their completion will enhance all life!"

Vinci and I were definitely not on the same page. He wanted to dump an agenda on me that I didn't need. But being an orphan for thirteen years had taught me how to handle jerks like him. I nodded, the same as if I got it. "You've been gone a long time, right? Like five hundred years?"

"Not 'gone,' Master. Searching for you."

"Whatever." He needed to be brought into the modern world. "The way it is now, *money* is where it's at. You could dress up like a baby kangaroo, put suction cups on your fingers, and walk up walls and across ceilings like a spider. Or—"

He started spinning out words like he was mad at me. "Young Master, do you not yearn to understand all things? The movements of oceans, the wonder of light, the sheer magic in the mundane?"

"No. What're you talking about?"

"Contemplate for a moment the wondrous marvel of digestion, the odyssey of the common potato."

What kind of a conversation was this?

"This most ordinary root is ground into small particles by one's teeth, and mixed and lubricated with bodily fluid. Then it travels through one's esophagus to a destination in one's stomach."

He wanted to talk philosophy or something. I wanted to get real.

"Thereafter, it is distributed throughout the whole of one's body. Miraculously, the body selects those nutrients from this root necessary to sustain its life. Simultaneously the body rejects that which it does not need. Furthermore, it has the amazing capacity to eliminate this excess!"

Right. Eliminate the excess. In other words, take a dump in the bathroom. What was so amazing about that?

"Can you not see that the process is a miracle? For how

can the body know what to select and what to reject? And that which one body rejects as waste product is thereafter used by other living beings as a nutrient. That is but one body, one life! There are an infinite number of lives on this Earth, each of which performs the miracle of digestion every day!"

Exactly. It all added up to a wondrous pile of excrement, otherwise known as— "So what?" I said. I didn't want to be rude to a hand so old it had age spots on it, but that stuff bored me. "If you can't sell it, what good is it?"

"Leonardo," he wrote. "This hand you see before you was, and is, the hand of Leonardo, the Master. And he is you."

That gave me another idea. "The guy who drew the Mona Lisa?"

He glared at me, then wrote, "Yes."

Sequels to the Mona Lisa! I could sell them at art auctions, the way I'd seen on TV. We'd go to New York, London, Paris, Tokyo, and Rome! *That* would bring in a few bucks! But I didn't want to scare him with too much. "How come you're still around?" I asked. "I mean the real Leonardo da Vinci died a long time ago, but here you are. That's a great trick."

"Young man, obviously you have not understood a word I have written. How does one account for the miracle of digestion?"

"One doesn't need to," I said, sarcastically. "It just *is*."

"As you say then, Master," it wrote. "And as am I."

This was stupid. Who cared about miracles? But Vinci wouldn't quit on the subject. "All life is a miracle, my boy," he wrote. "Clouds are miracles. Trees are miracles. The tiny insect, gifted with purpose and driven by need, is a miracle."

That meant there were a zillion miracles in the pig pen, buzzing around and biting the pigs and driving me crazy. "What I don't get is how you did it," I said. "I mean, you're only a hand and you're alive. How'd you get loose? How'd you stay alive for five hundred years?"

"My Master wished it. The Creator, the Prime Mover, the Giver of Life, for it matters not the name which is employed, did the rest."

"Leonardo da Vinci made a wish?"

"An inspired wish, my dear young man. Through a most wondrous insight, he foresaw the future. He knew his essence would return one day. And then, through some miracle of will, some transference of life, this old hand detached itself from his remains. I thus escaped death, and continue to live."

I didn't get it. But I'd seen weirder stuff on TV, such as flowers morphing into monsters. I quit trying to figure it out and focused on the possibilities. He could be worth more than the lottery. "You're my servant?" I asked him, one more time.

He did that stupid bow again. "I am indeed," he wrote. "You are my Master, and I am your most humble servant."

Twelve

I had this great idea. If Vinci was my servant, he'd do what I told him. What a concept. Move over, Bill Gates! Here comes Leonard Smith, thirteen-year-old millionaire! "Wait here," I said to him.

He tilted to one side and lifted his thumb, like body language. "Why?" the gesture asked.

"I'm hungry," I told him, remembering the apple pie Julie had baked last night. "I need to work a most wondrous miracle of digestion. Then we grab some necessities and we're out of here." The big necessity at that moment was money. Anna kept cash in a jar in the pantry. I wouldn't steal it exactly. It would be a loan she'd find out about after I borrowed the money. As soon as I made a killing, I'd pay her back. She'd understand. She needed money too, for Julie's back, Farley's lawyer, and the farm. If I got rich enough, I might lend her some. Man! I could taste what it must be like to be rich!

Vinci wrote me a note, asking where I planned to take him.

"New York! London!" I said. There were faster and better ways to make money than painting pictures, too. I'd teach him a few tricks! "Hollywood!" Ideas and plans flashed in my brain with perfect reception, like digital TV. "I'll hire an agent to set up a tour. Maybe get a recording contract. Do you do music? Play the drums, or the xylophone?"

He looked shocked, then started writing again.

"Later." I left the room, shutting the door behind me.

Julie sat at the kitchen table with her head in her hands. "Hi." She looked up at me and smiled.

Her eyes were red, so I knew she'd been crying. "Hi." I headed for the pantry. "You okay?"

"No. My back is killing me." She leaned forward in her chair like an old person, trying to move. "When I was nine, I could do three handsprings in a row and end it with a front flip."

"When I was nine I had three sets of foster parents, each one worse than the other." It was dark in the pantry so I turned on the light.

"It isn't in there," she said.

How did she know I was looking for the cash jar?

"It's on the counter by the bread box," she continued.

"What is?"

"The apple pie."

"Oh." I walked over and cut myself a big piece. Anna had put a list of chores next to it where I wouldn't miss it. No more chores for me, I thought. "Where's the old lady?" I asked.

"You've never called her *that* before."

"First time for everything." I sat down at the table.

"She went to see my dad." Julie laughed, but it came out like a groan. "How many kids do you know whose dads are in jail?"

"Lots," I told her. "If they aren't, they ought to be."

"Well, it's humiliating. It's bad enough the way kids treat us now, like when they hold their nose when they see us." She demonstrated. "Now this. I won't even be able to go to the mall. What if someone sees me?"

"Come on, Julie." I forked a big piece of pie in my mouth. "It isn't like a tattoo on your forehead that says, 'My old man's a convict.'"

"What if I never see him again? I mean, he did it for me. He could have been killed when he robbed that bank."

"I don't think so." The pie tasted great. I cut a piece of cheddar cheese to go with it. "Not with a toy pistol. He couldn't even shoot himself in the foot."

"He loves me, Nard. Now I may never see him again."

"That'd be soon enough for me."

"Who were you talking to?" she asked.

"What?"

"I heard you talking to someone." She leaned her elbows on the table and smiled at me. "It's okay. I won't tell anyone."

"Just myself." I wasn't about to tell her about my gold mine. "I do that sometimes when I wake up. What did I say?"

"You were going to get someone a new dress. I didn't know you had a girlfriend."

"I don't." I stuffed the last of the pie in my face. "When's the next bus for town?"

"Ten-oh-seven. You're not going anywhere. You have chores."

10:07! I had to hurry. I pushed away from the table and was in the pantry before Julie could move. "Anna won't mind if I take enough for the bus and a little extra, will she?"

"Nard! What are you doing?"

"This is important." Three twenties, a ten, a five, some ones, and change. I left the five and grabbed the canvas shopping bag she kept in there.

"Put it back! The shopping bag too!" I heard Julie struggling as she tried to stand up, then blew by her for my room. "*Nard!*" she screamed at me. "You've taken all the *money!*"

It didn't take long to pack. I tossed my clothes and

books in my backpack. But where was Vinci, my ticket off the stupid pig farm and into the world of my dreams?

I spotted him, crouched on a corner of the table, on all fives. "Hop in, humble servant," I ordered, opening up the bag. "We've got places to go and things to do!" But Vinci ignored me. "Hey," I said. "Get in the bag!"

He waggled from side to side. His way of saying "no."

"Come on, you creep!" I yelled at him, opening the shopping bag wider. "We have to catch the bus!"

"I *knew* you had someone in there!" Julie shouted. I heard her stomping down the hall. "Who is she?"

"You don't want to know." I sensed disaster and slammed the door shut. Vinci had picked up the pencil and started writing on a clean piece of paper. He jabbed at the sheet like the pencil was a spear.

"Oh, yes I do!" The door banged open. "Where— *WHAT IS THAT?*"

Vinci dropped the pencil. He kind of stared at Julie like a statue made out of ice.

I moved in front of the table, hiding him from her, willing him to disappear. "Just a fake hand I got from the telephone company," I said. "You know, let your fingers do the walking?"

"I saw a *real hand*, just *standing there*, on your *desk!*"

"Where?" I asked her, stepping out of the way.

But my stupid servant had not taken advantage of the chance to hide. He stayed on the table and scribbled away on the paper. Julie stared at him like a kid who'd never seen such a huge bug. He gripped the paper and tugged it toward me.

When he moved, Julie watched with fascination. I grabbed the paper out of the Hand. "What's that?" she asked.

"A message." I was so steamed I wanted to flatten the little miracle.

"What does it say?"

"'Master,'" I read, angrily. "'I beg you to reconsider your actions. I have traveled too long and too far to watch you throw your life away.'" Great, I thought. He tells me he's my servant, then tries to run my life. "'In the meantime, would you be so kind as to introduce me to your friend?'" I slammed the paper on the table and glared at him. "O-kay. This is Julie Marne. She lives here." I turned to Julie. "This is Vinci, my servant. He says he was the Hand of Leonardo da Vinci, but that was five hundred years ago. Shake hands."

"I don't think so," Julie said. "I mean, I don't want to be rude or anything, but I'm not ready for that. Now what's he doing?" she asked me.

"Writing another note. He writes backwards because he's weird." Vinci handed me the new message, which I read out loud. "'It is indeed a pleasure to meet you, young lady. But are you in pain? Do I observe an awkwardness about your posture? Perhaps I can help, if my Master will allow it.' Heck, I don't care," I said, tossing the paper on the table. My great plans to go to New York and make a million bucks were in the toilet. "He doesn't know squat about backs, though. All he ever did was a few paintings and some screwball inventions that never got off the drawing board."

Vinci picked up the pencil and crawled on the paper like a big spider. "I have dissected many human cadavers, at grave risk to my personal safety and well-being. Had I been discovered, I would have been burned at the stake. But in so doing, I have observed the wondrous mechanisms at work beneath the skin. I am also possessed of the special sensitivity of a healer. It may be immodest of me to confess to such powers, but quite true."

Julie warmed up to the creep. She stood by the table. "How would it help me?" she asked me. "I mean, I've been to the doctor and there isn't anything he can do except operate."

That set Vinci off again. We both said the words as he wrote them. "'I would explore the tissues, muscles, cartilage, tendons, and bones of your back with my fingers.'"

"Oh no." Julie folded her arms in front of her. "Not *my* back. It's a man's hand and an old man's hand at that. He isn't touching *me* unless he's a doctor."

He tilted, like a hand that didn't get it.

"She doesn't trust you, Vinci," I explained. "She thinks you're a dirty old hand."

He went right back to work. "Master, you may assure Julie that I am far beyond such concerns. At 500 years, one loses interest in such matters. But I am still driven by curiosity and an insatiable desire to understand all things."

"What is there to understand?" Julie asked me. "There's something wrong with my back. *He's* the one who's hard to understand. He writes backwards and uses nerdy expressions from the last century. I mean he *seems* nice, but you hear all this stuff all the time about, well, you know."

We both read what he wrote next. "My dear Julie. Experience is the great teacher, and it has taught me that God makes few mistakes. Before accepting that He made one in your case, I would examine you myself. For experience has also taught me that doctors are more prone to error than God.

"As to your other questions, I write in this manner because I am a left hand. I wish to see the words as I write them, rather than cover them with my hand. Devious motive can be attributed to the practice but the simple fact is, it is efficient. And be not frightened over my manner of expression. My mother gave birth to me in the Year of Our Lord 1452, a time when the metaphors were quite different. They had an elegance which seems to have been lost in the common discourse of this age. As hard as I try, it is impossible for me to be 'hip.'"

"What's 'hip'?" I asked Julie.

"You know. Cool." She looked like she was thinking things over. "Would I have to take off my clothes?" she asked. "I mean, for him to examine me?"

"That is the preferred manner of examination," he wrote, "for the very good reason that—"

"No way. Tell him if he tries that, I call the police."

"Be not afraid, young woman. I only offer my services, but if you question my motive then that is the end of the matter."

A car drove into the yard and I looked out the window. Anna and Farley were climbing out of the pickup.

What else could go wrong with my day? "Hey 'servant,'" I said, sarcastically. "Since you're such a do-gooder and want to fix people up, here comes a real challenge. He's Julie's dad. See if you can fix his brain."

Thirteen

"Daddy's back!" Julie lifted off like a space ship, blasted out of my door, and skipped down the steps as if nothing was wrong with her back.

Vinci got busy again. "Master, I beg of you," he wrote, "do not reveal my presence! I am not understood by..."

"Julie?" Farley hollered, banging his way into the house. "Where are you, honey?"

"...older persons," Vinci wrote, "I know not why. You must persuade young Julie to say nothing of me. I am adept at cloaking my presence from adults, primarily because they refuse to see what they do not understand. But I shall remain nearby so that I may assist you when you have a need for my services."

"Great," I muttered, wondering if I could turn him in

to the police. If there was a reward out for him, I might make a few bucks.

It was like he could read my mind. "Stay a moment, Master?" he wrote.

How does a thirteen-year-old kid say no to a 500-year-old hand? I turned toward him.

"I discern a measure of exasperation in your manner. Are you vexed with me?"

What did he mean by that? Pissed off? "Darn right I am," I said. "You told me you were my servant, but you don't follow orders. *I'm* the one who gets bossed around."

"Young Leonardo, you are still a boy," he wrote. "I am but a hand, yet I am wiser by 500 years. Be not impatient with me, for I know more of you than you do. Neither your modest origin nor your station in life are reflective of your immeasurable value. I would guide you toward the everlasting greatness which is yours to achieve. As your loyal servant, I must act in your *true* interest, even at the risk of incurring your displeasure."

More garbage for me to swallow. I heard Julie coming up the stairs, talking to her dad. "He writes notes," she said. "Only he's left-handed? So he writes them backwards!"

"I never heard the like of that," Farley said.

They bustled into my room. "There! See?" Julie said, pointing at Vinci.

He slid off the table top.

"I don't see anything," Farley said.

"He's under the table!" Julie bent down and looked under. "He's hiding! There he goes!"

Vinci streaked under my bed.

"That's crazy," Farley said. "I don't see anything."

"But Daddy, you have to look under the bed!"

"Honey baby, you're seeing things. You're worryin' too much and that's my fault. I haven't made it easy. At all."

"We've been robbed!" Anna screamed from the kitchen. In two seconds flat, she ran up the steps and into my room. "Somebody's been in the cash jar and this is all they left!" She waved a five-dollar bill.

"I, well, you see..." I tried my hardest to think of a good lie, but nothing came into my brain.

"Nard took it," Julie said.

My throat dried out and I swallowed, but couldn't talk. Anna looked like she'd been zapped with a stun gun. "You did?" she asked, huge disappointment on her face.

"See..."

"Those boys were back," Julie said. "They tied up at the dock. Nard took the money out of the cash jar to keep them from taking it. We just knew that's what they were after, Auntie."

"You left five dollars," Anna said to me, puzzled. "Why didn't you take all of it?"

I cleared my throat again. "See, the reason I did that..."

All the blood in my body had pushed into my face.

"He wanted them to find something," Julie said. "I mean, otherwise they'd have torn the house down."

What a lifesaver. I took the money out of my pocket and handed it to Anna.

She counted it and smiled with relief. "Seventy-two dollars and thirty-five cents," she declared. "I'm proud of you, boy. I knew I could trust you. It'll go right back where it was." Then she saw my pack, loaded with all my stuff, and the shopping bag. "You wasn't leavin' us, was you Nard?"

"Oh, no'm. I . . ."

"He wanted to get a job to help out," Julie said, "but wasn't sure what to wear. So he packed up his clothes."

"Lord knows we could use the money," Anna said, but rubbed her jaw, still wondering about something. "Let's see now. Did he pack up before, or after, those boys tied up at the dock? And what did he need with my shopping bag?"

"Before?" Julie asked, kind of a question.

"It happened so fast," I said. "I don't remember when I packed." I felt rotten lying to that old lady. I'd rather lie to Mrs. Cousins, which had been hard enough.

Anna put her arm around me, making it worse. "It don't matter," she said. "Just so we all know we can count on each other in a pinch. Can we count on you, Nard?"

"Yes!" I said. Julie smiled at me and so did Farley, and Anna gave me a big squeeze.

I meant it when I said it, too. How was I to know how things would work out?

Later that day I saw Julie alone. "Thanks," I said. "You really saved me. I was dropping through space without a parachute."

"It was easy," she said. "Girls are better liars than boys."

Maybe she was right. I hadn't thought about it. "Vinci..."

"Is that what you call him?" she asked. "Not 'Mister' or 'Doctor' or anything. Just Vinci?" I nodded. "Where is he?"

"Around. Don't tell Anna or Farley about him, okay? He says old people don't understand."

"I don't either," Julie said. "I just think he's cute."

Cute? I didn't argue with her, though. I had to work off my guilty conscience. I did all the chores on Anna's list, then weeded the vegetable garden and cleaned up the tack room. It didn't do much good. When Anna put her arm over my shoulder and told me what a fine young man I was, I felt guilty all over again.

After dinner we moved into the living room. Farley turned on the television to see if he'd made the news. He sat next to Anna on the couch while Julie and I sprawled on the floor.

The lead story wasn't about Farley. "Have you ever wanted to fly like a bird?" Polly Chan, the anchorperson, asked. Her face faded into a picture of some guy soaring over Table Mountain on a hang glider. "One of Mankind's oldest dreams got a boost today when Mayor Webb announced that Eldorado will host a human-powered flight contest." The guy cruised around in the sky. "It will be sponsored by CUTA!, for 'Clean Up The Air!'"

The hang glider swooped down like a condor, gliding toward us, then landing in a meadow. The wind jerked it forward a few feet, but the pilot got the big wing under control and waved.

Polly Chan showed up on the screen again. "CUTA! is a national foundation," she said, "started by the American Heart and Lung Association. It gets most of its money from billionaire Glen Turner. Mr. Turner's father lived in Los Angeles all his life, was not a smoker, but still died of lung cancer. Turner blamed his father's death on air pollution."

"So what is the contest about?" the weatherman asked.

"Human-powered flight." Polly Chan flapped her arms like wings. "The way birds do it, without motors."

The screen cut to a picture of what looked like an insect with long, thin wings and a short body. A man sat in the body on a bike frame, dripping with sweat, hunched over and pumping his legs like crazy. A propeller was mounted in the back. "It's been done, of course. In the *Gossamer Albatross*," Chan said. "The *Gossamer Albatross*, pictured here, flew across the English Channel in 1979. Then in 1988, a Greek cyclist flew in one like it from the isle of

Crete to the village of Santorini, on the mainland. A distance of seventy miles."

I felt a tug on my pantleg.

Vinci! What did he want me to do? Pick him up?

He nodded toward the TV, like telling me to watch, then slid under the couch.

"...not real practical, would you say, Polly?" the weatherman asked. The camera cut to his deadpan expression, like, "get it?" "Ford and GM and Chrysler aren't threatened, are they? People won't jump in their flying machine to go shopping, or go to work, or see a movie?"

Polly laughed. "True, which is the reason for this contest. CUTA! is looking for practical solutions to the problems of human-powered flight. And according to the announcement from the Mayor's office, big money will go to the winner."

"How much?"

"One hundred thousand dollars."

All of us perked up at that. "Turn that thing down," Anna said to Farley as she whipped through the paper, looking for something she'd seen. "Here it is." She showed it to me.

An article told the whole story, with pictures and an application blank. "You made that pig-feedin' wheel, Nard. I been studyin' the way you do things with just one hand. You don't suppose..."

Then she jumped up. Her face twitched, out of control.

"I'll be all right." She stumbled out of the room, but I could hear her snuffling in the kitchen. "About as much chance as winnin' the lottery," she mumbled, "and the money'd belong to him anyway. Now Anna girl, you keep yourself in one piece!"

I stared at Julie, who stared at me. Farley glared at the floor with a red face. A monster sniff came from the kitchen, big enough to pull plaster off the wall. "What's got into you, girl?" We could hear her talking to herself. "Now go out there with your back straight and your chin up and a smile on your face." She blew her nose, enough to fill a towel.

Then she marched into the living room like Joan of Arc in front of her army, with her chin up and a smile on her face.

Man, I thought. What a tough old lady.

Fourteen

I went to bed early. For the heck of it, I took the newspaper article with me and spread it on my desk. "'Night, Nard," Julie said, sticking her head in my room. "Is Vinci here?" she whispered.

"No."

I shut the door, sat down at my desk, and re-read the article. My "servant" would show up if he felt like it.

CUTA! had many approaches to follow for clean air. Human-powered flight was one of their strategies. I didn't care about the others and skipped to the human-powered flight contest.

It would be held annually, the article said, on the third weekend of August. The Mayor of Eldorado was all for it because Glen Turner and CUTA! predicted over a hundred entrants from all over the world. The mayor said the event could grow into something big, like the Super Bowl.

Eldorado had been picked because of its altitude. The earlier airbikes needed the dense air of sea level to fly, but CUTA! wanted to prove human-powered flight was possible anywhere...when Vinci started crawling up my leg. "Hey!" Having a hand crawl up your leg takes getting used to. "Warn me next time, okay?"

I stuck my stub down and he grabbed it like he belonged there. I put him on the table. He started walking back and forth over the article. "Is that how you read?" I asked.

He waggled himself, kind of a nod, and kept on reading. I read along, too.

The rules would be different each year, but the first year they were simple, even though they took up a whole column.

The aircraft couldn't cost more than four thousand dollars for parts and materials. "No problem there," I said to him. "We don't have any money anyway."

The wingspan at its widest point could not exceed twenty feet. The early airbikes had wingspans of seventy!

No batteries allowed, even solar-powered ones. All the power had to come from the operator.

The course would start on Table Mountain, then go northeast 12 miles to Greeley Lake, then south 13 miles to Eldorado Park, then northwest 12 miles, back to Table

Mountain. The total distance was 37 miles and first prize—a hundred thousand dollars!—would go to whoever did the loop in the least amount of time.

There was an application blank at the bottom of the page. I read it over. It cost a hundred dollars to enter, nonrefundable, and even after paying the entrance fee, you still might not be allowed to compete. An inspection committee could disqualify you if it found your aircraft was unsafe, could not possibly work, or had a power source other than the operator, like a hidden motor.

A big waste of time I thought, even though some neurons flashed in my brain. I started seeing pictures of ideas. Could a hang glider be driven through the sky?

Somebody would have thought of it. Hang gliders weren't cheap, either.

Vinci picked up a pencil to write me a note. "Young Master, human-powered flight fascinated Leonardo da Vinci," he wrote. "He devoted his inventive genius to the riddle, but never solved it. Yet his vast experience is here, in my fingertips. Does not the prospect of flying from cloud to cloud with the ease of a bird excite you?"

I yawned and scratched the back of my ear with my stub.

But what if I came up with a really cool invention? Alexander Graham Bell dreamed up the telephone, and Thomas Edison invented the light bulb. After major brainstorms, they sure didn't live on pig farms.

I got ready for bed.

What a jolt! I'd been dreaming about flying when this great idea burst into my mind.

It was dark outside, but that didn't matter. I bounced out of bed and hustled over to my desk, totally awake. Snapping on the light I grabbed some paper and tried to draw the flying cycle that buzzed around in my head.

My right hand butchered the vision. All it can do are stick figures. What I wanted to sketch out was as clear in my mind as a photograph, but it looked stupid on paper, like the drawing of a four-year-old. I wadded it up, heaved it out of my sight, and tried again.

It was so simple. A hang glider combined with a unicycle. The unicycle hung beneath the wing from a pole. The cyclist pedaled like crazy until he built up enough speed to lift off, then swung his feet up to a drive shaft with a propellor at the end of it! He still pumped away, but the unicycle wheel converted into a great big gear! The cyclist was no longer a cyclist. He'd become a pilot!

There were a million details to work out. The pole connecting the hang glider to the unicycle had to be rigid at first, but jointed so it could swing forward. And when the pilot made the swinging move, he'd be sitting on a patch of air. But the pole could attach to his back some way. When he swung his feet up, it could hook on to something hanging from the wing. The pilot would be like pedaling a recumbent bike.

I did more stick figures, wanting to get the ideas on paper before I forgot them. The big gear would have to drive a shaft that would turn the propeller. The knobby ridges of a mountain bike tire could be the cogs!

I don't know how long I worked on those stupid stick figures nobody could read except me. I had eight pages before my first big yawn, then my head settled down on the desk top, and I closed my eyes...

And was in a dream. There I was, two thousand feet above Bergen Lake, pedaling a flycycle.

The tall buildings in Eldorado are miles away. I see them through the brown cloud of pollution they're inside of, like a dirty bubble.

Speedboats in the lake below look like toys in a pond. The mansions around the lake are flat, like drawings.

There's Anna, feeding pigs. She waves at me, but my hands are working the levers over my head and I can't wave back.

That's how I know it's a dream. I have two hands.

I fly along the ridge of foothills to the south. I'm over the school. Kids who don't even know I exist are out there, waving at me.

There's Julie! She's real excited because she knows me. Kids who usually ignore her treat her like a celebrity!

An eagle glides by, checking me out. My legs work easily, effortlessly, as the propeller pulls me higher and higher into the sky. I waggle the wing, kind of like, "Hi, eagle."

Uh oh. He doesn't like me for some reason. His beady eyes glare at me like I'm invading his space.

Here he comes! He swoops in under the propeller and turns up like a rocket, ripping a big hole in the wing!

I fight the controls like crazy! But I tip to one side and am in a nose-dive! I try leveling out...when he rips through the wing again, tearing out another big hole!

Now what? I drop like a rock, right at a house that gets closer and closer and bigger and bigger, staring at...

"Nard boy. You all right?"

Anna! I'm on the floor, looking up at her. "Huh? Oh. Sure." My desk lamp was still on but it was getting light outside.

"You gave me a scare, honey. I saw your light on and peeked in and seen you on the floor with your legs twitching in the strangest way." She looked on the desk and picked up the stupid drawings. "My goodness Nard, I didn't know you could draw." She sat down and looked at them with excitement. "Would this thing work?"

I scrambled off the floor and looked at them. They were great! Exactly what had been in my mind.

Vinci must have drawn them. Somehow he'd figured out what I'd meant from those stupid stick figures. "I don't know," I said to Anna. "It sure would be fun to find out."

Fifteen

I woke up after eight. Anna always got me out of bed at six-thirty, but she must have let me sleep when she found me on the floor with my legs twitching. I dressed and stumbled down to the kitchen where everybody seemed to be waiting for me. Julie and Farley sat at the table and Anna was by the stove, cooking. "Who fed the pigs?" I asked, because that's what I should have done.

"Don't worry about the pigs," Anna said.

Farley had a mug of coffee in his hand and a frown on his face. Julie looked like she was busting to talk but wouldn't, for some reason. Anna brought me a platter of pancakes and bacon, then plopped two eggs in the skillet in bacon fat. The smells drove me crazy.

My drawings were spread out on the table, and Anna

glanced at them. "Do you think it will fly?" she asked me.

"I don't know." I put some bacon on my plate and two cakes, then loaded them with butter and honey. "I'd have to build it and see."

She nodded and worked the spatula under the eggs. Then something happened to her. She kind of caved in on herself, like someone had let out the air. "I can't do this," she said in a low voice. "I ain't got the temperament for it, and that's that." She splattered grease on top of the eggs, puffing up the white part like clouds.

"Can't do what?" I asked.

"Beg for help." I noticed then that neither Julie nor Farley had plates.

"What?"

"It's terrible of me, but I'm at my wits end and don't know what else to do."

My gosh. Did she want me to rob a bank?

"I'm ashamed of myself," she said. I was afraid she'd let the eggs stick to the pan but she got the spatula under them in time. "You don't owe me the time of day, Nard. You just forget what I was goin' to ask you to do."

How could I forget what I didn't know in the first place? She brought the eggs over and laid them on top of my cakes...when it dawned on me. She wanted me to enter that contest and win the prize money for her. "Hey," I said, thinking about food instead of big bucks. "I can't build it by myself." I forked an egg and the yellow part oozed into the cakes. They tasted even better than they smelled.

Anna put the skillet on the stove. "If all of us was to pitch in and help," she said, "you don't suppose—" She didn't say any more, but I knew what she meant.

I wasn't thinking right just then. "Hey. Take it all." The cakes were soaked with egg yolk and mushy with butter and honey, and it must have affected my brain. "What do I need money for anyway?"

That gnarled old hand of hers slid toward mine, then stopped. "You think on it," she said and got up.

"I don't need to," I told her. "I just want to build it. It'd be fun."

"Hot dang!" Farley said real loud, whipping a fist through the air. "Hot *dang!* You can count on me, boy! I got the summer off!" He sounded happy about it. "The railroad won't take me back until them robbery charges get taken care of."

"Nard, I knew you would, I knew you would!" Julie was all pumped, too. It put a lump in my throat, but didn't bother my appetite. "You'll need a business manager. I'll be your pilot too. I just *know* I can ride a unicycle!"

"Come on, Julie. I get to fly it."

"You can't, Nard. You've only—"

She had a point. The controls would take two hands.

"Julie," Anna said, "didn't we already talk about that? All the deciding gets done by Nard."

"I know Auntie, and I promise to do exactly what he says, but he *likes* talking things over with me because it gives him ideas. Don't you, Nard?"

I nodded. My mouth was full and it was easier to nod than disagree with her.

"I got some ideas too, boy," Farley said.

Uh oh.

"Well, praise the Lord." Anna glowed like the moon on a clear night. "I'll figure up some way to get that hundred dollar entrance fee. How much money will it take to get started?" she asked me.

"Gosh, I don't know."

"I'm good at estimates, Nard," Julie said.

"Maybe he don't want your help," Anna said.

"No. I could use it."

"All right, then." Anna had that determined look on her face. "Farley, come with me. We got the chores to do this morning. Julie, you clean up this mess so you and Nard can have a decent place to work."

"Nard has to help with the dishes," Julie said.

"No, he don't." She stuck her hand in my hair. "You're a fine young man, Nard. I never had any children, but you'd have done me just right."

I saw Vinci under the stove. He waved a thumb at me, as though he was proud we were related.

I realized I'd just given away a hundred thousand dollars.

We didn't have anything in writing. Am I as nice as she thinks, I wondered?

As soon as Anna and Farley were out of the kitchen, Vinci crawled out from his hiding place. "Don't think you're getting away with anything," Julie told me, pushing away from the table and going over to the sink. "You have to help clean up just as soon as you finish eating."

She almost stepped on him. "Look out," I said. "You almost stepped on my hand."

He scuttled out of the way. When Julie saw him she jumped sideways, then laughed. "Hi, Vince," she said. He stopped and faced her, kind of turning red. "What's wrong with him?" she asked me.

"It's Vinci," I told her, exaggerating the sounds. "He's very sensitive."

"Vinci?" she asked me, kind of leaning into it.

"Almost."

"Vinci." Her hands opened and her body puffed up just a scooch.

"Perfect," I told her. He spidered to the top of the table and nodded at us. "He needs paper," I said. "And a pencil."

"So get them. I'm doing dishes."

"Come on, Julie. I'm still eating."

"You're always eating." But she went to the living room and came back with them. "Here you are, sir," she said to Vinci.

"Sir!" I said. "How come?"

"Because he's five hundred years old."

He positioned the paper in the middle of the table, got on the right margin, and started scribbling away. "My dear Julie. You honor me by showing respect for my years," he wrote in that backwards way of his. "But I would be your friend, and would prefer that you call me 'Vinci,' as does Leonardo. And young man, to you I say this. I am privileged to be in the service of one so generous." He stopped and bowed at me. "On this day, you have exhibited the becoming nature and grace of the Master."

Not the time to tell him I'd changed my mind. "Thanks for the drawings."

"Did Vinci do those pictures?" Julie asked me.

"We kind of work together," I told her, pushing away the plate. "I have an idea and draw it sort of with my right hand, and somehow he knows what I mean. Watch." I picked up the pencil and did a stick figure diagram of an idea I'd had about handholds in the wing. Vinci knew right away what to draw, and in five seconds, did a sketch from directly in front and another from an angle that gave perspective.

"I am impressed," Julie said. "What's it for?"

I started to explain, but Vinci drew a picture of the pilot, rolling down the runway on his unicycle, holding the wing over his head. That one took about thirty seconds.

"That is so cool," Julie said. "Was it your idea or his?"

"Mine I think, but he blew that one out so fast I'm not sure."

He wrote, "Master, you are the brain. I am your servant. Use me well."

Why did he always have to stick a little moral on the end? I took my dishes to the sink and dropped them in the dishpan.

Julie tossed me a wet rag. "You can wipe off the table and stove," she said. "*He* may be your servant but *I'm* not."

It took two telephone calls for Julie to find out that hang gliders cost $3,000. Where would we get money like that? Maybe we could build one, but out of what? Something strong, light, and cheap. "Young Master, may your humble servant make a suggestion?" Vinci wrote.

"If you don't stop calling me 'Master' I'm going to squash you." The words just popped out. He was 500 years old and I may have hurt his feelings, but at that moment I didn't care.

"But you are—"

"I am not! You aren't my humble servant, either." It was time to clear the air. "You only do what you want to anyway, and involuntary servitude is unconstitutional. Okay?"

He sagged like he was dejected, then wrote, "Do you wish me to leave?"

"No. I like having you around because you're different."

"You don't have to be so mean," Julie said.

"Who's being mean? I'm setting him free!" I didn't need a 500-year-old conscience in my life, either. "You wouldn't like it if he called you 'Queen Julie' all the time."

"Make it 'Princess' and I could get very used to it."

"My prickly young man," Vinci wrote, "may I make my suggestion?"

"That's something else. Don't ask for permission all the time. You're almost five hundred years older than me, so you can do what you want."

"As you say." He wrote very slowly as he tried to get used to the new rules. "Let the fabric for the wing be made of silk, which is light and of exceeding strength. Fashion the frame around which the silk is configured of bamboo."

Julie read it too. "Great." She grabbed the telephone book and was flipping through the yellow pages when Anna and Farley banged into the kitchen.

"How are you children doing?" Anna asked, walking to the sink to wash her hands.

But Farley looked right at Vinci, who melted into the table and slid out of sight. Farley blinked, but you could tell he didn't believe it, whatever it was. He shrugged it off.

"We need a hang glider," I said, like nothing was wrong. "They cost three thousand dollars."

Anna stopped wiping her hands. "How much?"

"Plus another five hundred for—" I stopped talking. Both of them looked sick. "Could you borrow the money from—"

"No." She sat down. "I won't ask that man for any more."

"That's kind of what we thought too," I said, "so we're working on another plan. We'll build one out of bamboo and silk, the way Leonardo da Vinci did." Maybe that's what da Vinci used.

"Bamboo? Silk?" Anna asked, doubtfully.

"Will that work?" Farley asked. Even he had enough brains to wonder about it.

"I guess we'll find out," I said.

Sixteen

Half an hour later, Julie knew how much it would cost. Silk was too expensive, but nylon wasn't. It went for $2.85 a linear yard, which was five feet by three feet. Ten linear yards would be plenty. She also found an export-import place that sold bamboo poles at a dollar each. They came in six- to eight-foot lengths. Fifty poles would give us three hundred feet.

"You must allow room for error," Vinci wrote. "You may need more than one model. 'Tis better to have too much than not enough."

Who asked him? But we went with seventy poles and fifteen yards of nylon, then tacked on fifty dollars for incidentals. One hundred sixty-two dollars and seventy-five cents. "We'll need a unicycle too," I said. "Add two hundred bucks for that."

Julie looked discouraged. "That's three hundred and sixty two dollars and change. I don't think Anna has that much."

But Anna didn't even blink when we told her what it would cost. She and Farley put a cage in the bed of the pickup, herded in a prize pig, then drove off for the sale barn.

The poor pig. I decided not to think about it.

The minute they were gone, Julie disappeared into her room and came out with three twenty-dollar bills in her hand. "This is money I've saved since I was eight years old," she said. "For dancing lessons." Then she marched into the pantry and got the cash jar. "If you tell Aunt Anna on me, I will kill you." She took out the cash. "Dead."

"What are you doing?"

"I am going to be the pilot." She stomped out of the kitchen like the queen of the world...when something happened in her back. I watched her stagger to the couch in the living room and had to choke back a laugh. How could she be the pilot if she couldn't stand up?

But it wasn't funny. She was in serious pain. Her teeth gritted, and one hand groped for the sore spot. "Darn it! Oh-h! It *hurts!*"

Vinci zipped out of nowhere and scampered for the couch. He looked at me and thoughts passed between us, as plain as if we were talking out loud. "Roll over on your stomach," I told her.

"Why?"

"So I can rub your back."

She sobbed with pain, but did it.

"Tell me where it hurts." I put my hand on her back, about in the middle.

"Down."

I moved it down an inch or two. "There?"

"Keep going."

I didn't want to go any lower. It didn't seem right. But Vinci didn't care. He got right in the small of her back and danced on his finger tips.

"Ohhhh!" Julie said, sighing with relief. "Ohhhhh that feels good." She took some deep breaths. "A little lower."

He went a whole lot lower than was decent, then kneaded the muscles along her spine where they went into her bottom. He'd walk up a few inches then walk down, squeezing and punching and twisting along the way. "That is so great," she said, closing her eyes.

The money she'd been carrying had scattered all over the floor. I got down on my knees to pick it up.

"Nard, where did you learn to do that?" she asked, sleepily. "It is so cool. You're better than my physical therapist."

"Learn what?" I said from about ten feet away.

"That." Her eyes popped open. "Where are you?"

"I'm picking up the money you spilled all over the place."

"You mean—" I saw her tense up. Vinci felt it too and

got ready to bail out. "Oh, I don't care." She relaxed into the couch. "I've been compromised."

I guess there are worse things than being compromised. Julie went to sleep.

While Julie slept, Vinci and I went out to the barn. I tried to see me building a hang glider out there. There was a workbench in the tack room and old-fashioned carpenter's tools hung on the pegboard behind it, like chisels and mallets and hammers and saws and awls and clamps. Would I need power tools for a hang glider? Too bad if I did. It was early 1800s in the tack room. It hadn't been wired for electricity.

Anna and Farley drove into the yard while we were still out there, and Vinci dropped out of sight. Anna grinned like she'd just won the lottery. "That old porker fetched four hundred dollars!" she said. "Where's that list of things you need, Nard? Give it to Farley and he'll go fill it."

I went into the house to get it from Julie, but she wasn't there. She'd pinned a note to the couch.

Hi—it's me. My back feels wonderful, so please thank Vinci for me. I've gone shopping for a unicycle in case you're wondering. But don't tell Auntie if she and my dad get back before I do, okay? I saw an ad in the paper for a secondhand unicycle for $150,

but they'll take less. They'll have to because I don't
have that much. Later.

What did Julie know about unicycles? So she was the best gymnast at Bergen Middle. Did that make her an instant expert?

I found the list though, complete with addresses, what to ask for, and how much. I took it outside and gave it to Farley who waited in the truck. "Do you know where those places are?"

"Yup."

Anna counted out one hundred and eighty dollars and gave it to him. "You won't be long now, will you?" she asked him.

"Nope." He winked at me and drove off.

Farley had never winked at me before. It was like ...

Uh oh. I recognized the signs.

Farley'd had another brainstorm.

Seventeen

"I should have sold Farley instead of that pig!" Anna muttered. "The trouble of it is, he isn't *worth* anything!" It was after seven and dinner was in the warming oven, where it had been for over an hour. "What happens to that nephew of mine?" she asked. "And his daughter. Where could they be?"

"Maybe it's genetic," I said.

"I don't care if it is. A grown man ought to have enough sense to use the telephone! Don't he know the trouble he could get in? And Julie! A young girl should know better than to go off into town by herself! Where could she be? She don't have any money, so...You don't suppose..."

Anna zipped into the pantry and found the cash jar.

It was empty but had a note in it. "IOU $77.65. Julie Marne."

She slumped down at the kitchen table. "You go on outside and leave me be, boy. I got to think on this, and maybe pray some, too."

The sun was ready to drop out of sight, and the sky to the east had filled up with clouds. They looked like someone had painted them red. It was so quiet I could hear the bus grind to a stop on the highway, half a mile away.

I really felt sorry for Anna, but I'd been thinking too. I went to the tack room, expecting to find Vinci, but he wasn't there. The drawings were on the workbench.

I liked the way they pictured my flycycle. Each one showed a new angle and explained a different detail of construction. You could see how the unicycle held up the wing when it was on the ground, rolling forward and building up speed. When the wing lifted into the air, the unicycle hung underneath like a pendulum. The pilot would swing the wheel forward until it hooked into a drive shaft that turned the propeller. Now the wheel became a great big gear. When the pilot pedaled the wheel, instead of rolling along the ground, it spun the propeller and pulled him up, up, up into the sky.

But I'd read about inventors with great ideas who died in the poorhouse. Some sold out for a song to someone else who made a fortune. Others had their ideas stolen. A few gave them away, just as I had.

Why had I been so stupid? I wanted to get rich! I should take care of myself before I took care of other people.

"Nard?"

Julie! I dropped the drawings and ran outside. "Where've you been? You'd better tell Anna you're—"

She was balanced on top of a unicycle! Her feet were on the pedals and her arms spread out like the wings of a big bird. "See?" She looked as comfortable and relaxed as a cowboy sitting on a horse. "You either have it or you don't. That's what the boy who sold it to me said, and I've got it! You just *have* to let me be the pilot!"

"Heck, anybody can do that. You've been practicing."

"Just today. I'll bet *you* can't."

Anna came outside. "Julie?"

"Look at me Auntie! Wheeeee!" She rode around in a circle.

Anna watched with her mouth open. "That's just plain amazing. You know, your mamma could walk on clothes lines when she was a girl." She looked at me. "You don't suppose it's genetic do you, Nard?"

"No'm." If Julie could do it, so could I. "Let me try, okay?"

I got on.

Wham! Face plant, right in the dirt! I tried again.

Splat! The wheel couldn't wait to roll forward, tossing me to the ground.

"How do you get the seat to stay still?" I asked Julie.

"You just don't think about it."

The two of them tried to hold me up, but it was like sitting on top of a ball that was balanced on a bigger ball. The seat wouldn't stay in one place. I still splattered my face in the dirt. It would take me a hundred years to learn to ride it.

When it started to get dark I went inside. Anna wanted me to stay outside with her and listen to crickets, while Julie practiced on her new toy. But I had to be alone. They had tried not to laugh when I'd crashed and burned, but they couldn't help it. I hated being laughed at. I told them I'd sit by the telephone in case Farley called up from somewhere.

Inside, I flipped through the yellow pages of the phone book. "Inventors Protection Agency" was listed under Invention Services. The ad said, "Ideas, Inventions, New Products. Protect Your Invention Before You Lose It!"

So I couldn't ride a dumb unicycle. I'd rather ride in luxury cars and Learjets any day. I decided to call Inventors Protection Agency as soon as I had the chance.

Just before ten o'clock, way after dinner, we heard the truck roll in. Everybody ran outside in time to see Farley miss the corner of the porch by half an inch. He slammed on the brakes and jerked his way out of the cab. There should have been a big roll of cloth in the bed of the pickup and stacks of bamboo poles, but there wasn't anything.

He smelled like his clothes had been washed in whiskey. "Turn on the television," he said.

"Where have you been?" Anna demanded, but he brushed by her with a small sack in his hand. "Are you drunk?"

"I been thinkin' is what I've been doin'," he said "Whiskey helps me to think. Turn on the Channel Four news." We followed him into the living room and watched him lurch toward the television set and flip it on. "That boy needs a real hang glider, not some flap-doodle thing made out of bamboo and silk."

They announced the winning lotto number on Channel Four news at ten o'clock. "What did you do with the money for the supplies?" I asked him because Anna couldn't. She'd propped herself up against the wall and couldn't talk.

"What we should'a done right from the start," he said, plopping on the couch. He lifted the sack up and shook it. "Know what's in here? One hundred and fifty chances to win the lotto! With odds like that, we can't lose!"

Anna slid down the wall, onto the floor.

The winning lotto number was "Eight and that's followed by a twenty-one and next we have a twenty-eight and then here comes a thirteen and a thirty-three and our final number tonight is forty-seven."

"Find it for me, honey," Farley said to Julie. "It's in here somewhere." Then just like that, he fell asleep.

We took the sack to the kitchen and spilled the tickets on the table. Farley hadn't even known what he'd bought. Half were lotto tickets, but the rest were for some game called "Perfecto." We separated the tickets into two piles and went through them. My hand sweated with excitement because each one could turn us into millionaires. Anna staggered in and watched our faces like a poker player looking for signs.

The winning ticket wasn't there. The miracle didn't happen. "Auntie, I'm so sorry," Julie said.

Anna pasted a smile on her face and stuck her hand in Julie's hair. "Don't let it worry you, child. There's still two hundred and twenty dollars left and this boy can work miracles." She smiled at me, then marched into the living room. "Farley!" she yelled. "Git up off that couch!" We heard a thud when Farley hit the floor and a minute later he came running through the kitchen with Anna chasing after him, whacking him with the fireplace broom.

"Nard. Julie." He nodded at us as he ran for the door. "Believe I'll sleep outside tonight."

Eighteen

The next morning, I had my chance. The fence had been cut the night before and I'd been helping Anna and Farley mend it. Anna sent me to get water and fruit to snack on.

Once in the house, I grabbed the telephone and dialed the number in my brain. "Inventors Protection Agency," a man's voice said.

"Hi. Uh, well, I've got an idea about a flying hang glider, and—"

"Out with it kid, I don't have all day. What's your idea?"

"It's a combination unicycle and hang glider? What happens is when you get off the ground, the unicycle wheel converts into a gear that turns the propeller."

"Maybe it's worth something, depends. What have you got? Diagrams, drawings, descriptions—the three 'Ds'—is what you need to prove ownership. Does this have anything to do with that CUTA! contest?"

"Sort of. If we have it built in time to enter."

"You'd better hurry on down here. Know where my office is?"

I knew Eldorado like the back of my hand. "Sure, but—"

"You have a serious problem, kid. Once you enter the contest, that idea is in the public domain. Then it isn't yours anymore. It belongs to anyone who wants to use it."

"Gosh."

"Take my advice and get down here before someone steals your idea. When can I see you?"

I heard Julie in the hall upstairs. "Soon," I said, and hung up.

"Hi, Nard," Julie said. She had to lean on the bannister to get down the stairs. She'd been on the unicycle too long the day before and hadn't been able to get out of bed. "Who were you talking to?"

"Some guy I used to know. Where are the apples?" I felt like a spy with a secret when I went back outside.

An hour later, Julie came running out the door. "Auntie! Daddy! Nard! Come quick!"

"What is it, child?" Anna asked.

"Daddy won some money!"

I almost let go of the fence spreader, which would have leveled Farley. Anna dropped her shovel. "How much?"

"Three thousand nine hundred and forty-eight dollars!"

"Oh my." Anna sat on the ground.

It took Farley a minute to understand. "You mean I done somethin' that worked out right?" he asked me

"Yes!"

He took a big patch of air into his lungs, and smiled.

One of the Perfecto tickets had won! He hadn't hit the jackpot, but there was enough to buy a hang glider.

We quickly finished the splice, then Anna made us kneel on the ground and say our thanks. My heart wasn't in it. Now we could buy a hang glider and win the contest, but there went my rights to the idea. It would soon be in the "public domain," whatever that was.

Anna took charge of the winning ticket, and she and Farley drove off to get the money. It must have made Julie's back feel better because she jumped on her unicycle and trained.

I had to go into action, and the sooner the better. The heck with the money from the dumb contest. I had to protect my rights to the idea. The trouble was, I couldn't stop thinking about how bad Anna needed the money. She could pay Mr. Robinson back, and wouldn't have to sell the farm to him. She could pay for Julie's back operation too.

But winning it wouldn't do *me* any good. If my flycycle

invention was good enough to win a hundred thousand dollars, it might be worth a million.

I slid into the barn to get my drawings...

They were gone! I'd left them on the workbench in the tack room. Where were they?

Julie was in the yard, riding the unicycle. "Hey Julie, did you see my drawings?"

"No," she said. "Watch." She leaned to one side far enough to fall, but turned into it and kept her balance. "Why?"

"I need them."

"Ask Vinci. This is so much fun! I'm getting good at it, too."

Did Vinci have them? "Doesn't all that riding hurt your back?" I asked Julie.

"No. He's been..." She blushed.

"He compromised you again, didn't he?"

"He massaged my back, if that's what you mean."

"When?"

"This morning, after I was wide awake and completely dressed."

"If you see him, tell him I want my drawings."

I went back to the tack room to look again. Vinci was on the workbench waiting for me, standing on a blank sheet of paper, holding a pencil in his fingers. "Where are they?" I asked. He didn't move. "You know where they are, don't you?"

He waggled himself, kind of a nod, that meant "yes."

"Get them. They're mine. I need them."

"My dear young fellow," he wrote, "I would save you from your baser instincts. You know not the harm and destruction you would wreak on yourself, and those who love you, in the pursuit of personal gain. I cannot allow this to..."

"Get them before I flatten you."

"...occur. You are but a young man without the wisdom of..."

I took the mallet from the pegboard, mad enough to splatter him all over the room.

"...five hundred years. One day you will..."

I swung the mallet down with all my strength. He skipped out of the way. The mallet mashed into the bench and bounced out of my hand.

"...thank me for interfering in your affairs. You see, we are connected through the spirit. Your thoughts..."

I picked the mallet up out of the dust and tried again and missed again. Man, he was quick.

"...run through me as you think them. I would be your counselor and advisor until..."

There was a shovel in the corner. I'd dig a hole and put him in it.

"...you are of an age to be trusted with the enormity of your gifts. For they are gifts from the Creator of All Things, and you must..."

I tried hitting him with the shovel but that didn't work either.

"...guard them and employ them in the service of..."

"Nard?"

Julie stood in the doorway to the tack room. "Hi." I tried to sound cool.

"...mankind." He stopped writing and bowed at me, like my obedient servant.

"What are you doing? Why all the noise?"

"We were just talking."

"Some conversation. What about?" She looked at me. "Are you mad at him?" I started to cry. "Nard, are you okay?" she asked.

I ran out of there. It had been bad enough to fall flat on my face in front of Julie. I didn't want her to see me cry.

Nineteen

Early the next day, with $3,948.00 in the bank, Anna drove Julie and me to Air Adventure Hang Gliders to buy a hang glider. It was in the foothills fifteen miles north of the pig farm.

The office was in the back of a hangar. Five gliders hung from the ceiling. Three looked like huge brightly colored butterflies. The other two were like painted birds with outstretched wings, soaring in the sky.

A thin man who looked like a bicycle racer with muscles made out of rope came up to us. "Hi, I'm Mack Rogers."

We told him our names, and then Anna took out her checkbook. "We'd like to buy a hang glider from you," she said.

He smiled. "Does one of you have a license?" That's when we found out he only sold to pilots with licenses to fly. "Too dangerous," Mack said. "It's for your own good."

"How do you get a license?" I asked.

"I have a school starting Monday. It takes a week. But I have an age requirement, and you probably don't qualify." He grinned at Anna. "*You* would," he told her.

"Heavens." She looked at the ceiling where the gliders kind of floated over the floor. "You wouldn't get me up there."

"I'd be the one to take the class," Julie said. "I'm thirteen but very mature for my age. I'll be fourteen in October."

Mack frowned, thinking. "Girls usually are well enough coordinated at thirteen, but I don't like training anyone under sixteen. There isn't any law though, and if your parents consent to it—" He shrugged. "It's possible."

"How risky is this?" Anna asked.

"Nowhere near what most people think," Mack told her. "It's a judgment sport. People with good judgment don't have much to worry about. But hot-dogs do. They get hurt, and worse." Worse than hurt, I thought? Dead? "There's something about flying, too," he continued. "When you're in the sky, there's nothing like it. Just being there can change the way you think."

"Auntie, I've got good judgment," Julie said, looking at the ceiling. "I'd be really, really careful."

"Honey, I've seen you cuttin' up on a unicycle. Are you sure?"

"Yes!"

Mack looked interested. "She rides a unicycle?"

"As good as you'll see in a circus," Anna told him.

"She isn't very big," Mack said. "She'd have to be able to pick up a hang glider." At the far end of the hangar he had one on the ground. "Let's see how strong you are."

We walked over to it. Its colors were bright enough to light up a dark room. It sat on little wheels and a tail, like a tricycle. The wheels were at the bottom of a big "A" about five feet tall. The tip of the "A" stuck like the point of an arrow into the middle of the big wing, and a thin pole stuck above the wing like a periscope. Four wire ropes stretched off the top of the periscope and hooked into the wing, maybe to keep it from sagging down. There were wire ropes under the wing, too. They stretched off the ends of the crossbar of the "A" holding everything stiff.

"See if you can do this," Mack said to Julie. He ducked under, braced the side bars of the "A" on his shoulders, and stood up. The glider lifted off the floor. He trotted forward a few yards with those big wings on his back like a low-flying dinosaur. He leaned to one side and ran in that direction, did a loop, and came back. He was puffing when he set it down.

"Here goes," Julie said, getting under it. All I could

think about was her back. But she hoisted it off the ground and started running. "Like this?" she asked, running out farther than Mack had. When she leaned to one side for her turn, she started to lose her balance. "Whoops!" She ran fast enough to catch up with herself, did a loop, and came back. Carefully she set it down. Her face hurt, but she had a big grin on, too.

"How much do you weigh?" Mack asked her.

"Ninety-three pounds."

"That glider weighs sixty," he said. "You'd have to run down a slope with one of these on your back. Could you?"

"Not very far," she said.

"You wouldn't have to go very far," he told her. "Plus it gets lighter once you start running."

"It does?"

He nodded. "The air gets underneath the wing and lifts it up. Before you know it, you're off the ground."

"I'd be in the sky?" Julie asked, her face glowing and her eyes shining with excitement.

Mack turned to Anna. "She might be able to do it," he said. "It'd be great for the sport. There aren't enough women."

"Except he'd have to come to class with me." Julie motioned at me. "I mean, not to fly. Just to see what happens."

"That'd be all right," Mack said. "I could use the help."

The course cost $500 and a hang glider, $3,000. But if we bought it from Mack, the package would be $3,350.

I had some questions. All the hang gliders I saw were too big. "We need one that's only twenty feet across," I told him.

"Why so small?"

"For what we need, that's as big as it can be."

"If this is for that CUTA! contest, you're the seventh bunch who've asked me about it."

Other people had my great idea? "What did you tell them?" I asked.

"That there's no way a hang glider could fly around a course like that."

Anna put her arm around me. "Maybe this boy don't look it," she said, "but he has it up here." She tapped her forehead. "He just might have figured out how to do it."

Mack shrugged. You could tell he wasn't convinced. "What you do with the bird is your business," he said to Anna. "Selling it to you is mine."

"But if I pass the course you'll sell it to me, right?" Julie asked.

"Not a twenty-foot bird," he said. "They're too small and way too fast. The skill level needed to fly one is way beyond what I could teach you in a week."

"Even if I can do it?" Julie demanded. "I mean, I can ride a unicycle!"

That made him think. "Here's what I'll do. I'll order

one, but no sale until I'm convinced you can fly it. Fair enough?"

"So if you don't think I can fly a twenty-footer, you won't sell me one that size?" Julie asked. "Only a bigger one?"

"Yes."

"But that wouldn't do us any good!" she said.

"Go to another dealer then," Mack told her. "I'm not about to risk your life for a few bucks."

"My life?"

"Julie, if you catch a thermal lift and it takes you up ten thousand feet, then something happens that puts you in a dive and you come screaming into a building or a cliff, you're dead. I don't need that on my conscience."

Wow. He made it sound serious.

"Oh, my," Anna said. "Children, it's too risky. The money we could win isn't worth Julie's life! We'd best be—"

"Auntie?" Julie looked up at the gliders hanging from the ceiling like they were food and she was dying of hunger. "He said he wouldn't sell us one unless he's convinced I can fly it."

"That's right, honey."

"Let me try?"

There was something in Julie's face, like a fire that nobody could put out. Anna saw it, too. "You'd have to do everything just like he says," Anna said. "If he don't

think you can, then there's no argument. Are you willin'
to do it that way?"

"Yes," Julie said.

"Promise?"

"Oh, yes!" she said again. "I want to fly!"

Twenty

There were two other people in the flying school with Julie. One was an old guy with gray hair, the other a college student who looked like a movie star. They thought the girl would hold them back, but it was the other way around. They had trouble getting off the ground, but not Julie. Mack called her "Bird Girl" and told her she was a natural.

Mack made them fly the first morning. There was a hill, not very steep but over a hundred yards long, behind the hangar. The wind always seemed to blow up the hill, which Mack said was perfect for hang gliding.

The students carried training gliders to the top of the hill. Julie had trouble, but she made it. They held them by the control bar, which was what they called the big "A" under the wing. If you wiggled it, the wing wiggled.

Mack fitted them into their "harness," a big sling made of belts and stuff. When the glider was in the air, the pilot hung in the sky from the harness, under the wing. It was clipped to the "keel," which was the pole that stretched from the nose to the tail. The pointed end of the control bar was attached to the keel at the same point.

He faced them down the hill into the wind. They held the wing over their head like a big sail and ran down the hill. It was so cool! Julie was gliding over ground before she got thirty yards out, like an eagle, coming in for a landing.

Could my flycycle do the same thing? If the pilot didn't need a unicycle to get in the air, it could save some weight. The big gear that drove the propeller could be already there, hanging from the keel. Then once in the air, the pilot could swing her feet into the pedals.

I found out from Mack there were different styles of harnesses, depending on how the pilot liked to fly. Most wanted to zoom through the air with their face into the wind like Superman, but another style was made for pilots who liked lying on their back, as on a hammock. That style was called "suprone," and would be perfect for a flycycle. The pilot's feet would be right where they were needed to pump away.

It was cool, all the stuff I was learning. Like how to "see" the wind, its direction and velocity, even though there isn't anything to see. You see it by feeling it, the way birds do, or fish see currents of water in a stream. I learned about "turbulence," too. That happens when a current of air gets blocked, like from a building. Also why the wing is thick at the leading edge, then tapers down to a paper-thin surface. It creates "lift" by knocking air above the wing out of the way.

But when I told Mack about my great idea, he wasn't very encouraging. "It won't work, Nard," he said. "Ever hear of an ultralight?"

I'd seen one in a movie. A girl found a lost flock of geese in one. She led them to a lake in a city. "Yes."

"Most ultralights are just hang gliders with motors that drive the propeller. There's a whole body of technology about them. But they push the wing through the air from the rear."

"So?"

"Do it your way and you'll nose-dive."

"Why?"

He looked at me with patience, the way teachers do when you ask too many questions. "The center of gravity. It'll shift forward when Julie hooks her feet to the gear."

"What do you mean?" I asked him.

He drew a picture. "Here's the center of gravity," he said, "right in the middle of the keel. All the weight— that's the pilot in her harness and the control bar—hangs from one spot. As long as the wing stays at the right attitude, the glider flies level. You push the control bar forward to tilt the wing at an angle so she climbs, and you pull the control bar back to tilt the wing so she dives. See how that works?"

"Yes."

"If you load the nose with weight, she can't fly level. A gear, a drive shaft, and a propeller will add weight, and that will pull the nose down."

I looked at his sketch. "The center of gravity is like the balance point on a teeter-totter, isn't it?" I asked him.

"That's right."

"Can't a big kid balance on a teeter-totter with a little kid?" I drew a stick figure picture too. "If you move the little kid all the way to the end, and make the big kid sit closer to the teeter-totter point, they'll balance."

"What are you getting at?" he asked me.

"Why not put the pilot back far enough so she'd balance with the propeller and gear?"

He smiled and shrugged. "Possible I suppose, but there's another reason a hang glider won't work. Weight."

I'd thought about that a lot. Most hang gliders weighed fifty or sixty pounds, and Julie wasn't strong enough to fly something so heavy. "Why do they weigh so much?" I asked. "Can't they be made lighter?"

"Sixty feet of tubing for the frame is twenty pounds. Add the weight of fabric for the sail. Julie'd need a hundred and thirty-five yards, which would weigh thirty pounds." He shrugged. "There isn't a ninety-three-pound person in the world who can pull fifty pounds plus her own weight through air."

"Can the fabric be lighter?" I asked.

"No. It has an oil base and is tear-resistant. When you're four or five thousand feet above the ground, you need a material that can withstand the stresses. You don't want that wing made out of hankies."

"But she'd never get that high. I mean, that isn't what she'd be doing. She'd be like driving it…"

"There are lighter materials," he said, thinking of something. "Paragliders use a very light fabric. I wonder."

He had a computer that could do models and figure weights. We played around with different designs. The control bar had to stay where it was, at the center of gravity. But the pilot didn't have to be there. If the control bar had long handles, she could move back. Then the harness could hang from someplace behind the control bar and still balance the weight of the propeller, gear, and drive shaft.

And by using a lighter fabric for the wing, the tubing could be lighter too. Twenty-five pounds could be lopped off. Was Julie strong enough to pull thirty pounds of glider through the sky?

"You know something?" Mack said, stroking his jaw. "This could work."

———

"Those boys shot a dog!" Anna said one night, driving us home from the school.

"You mean Erik, Mikey, and Fish?" I asked.

"It was in the paper," she said. "A new burglary in Bergen Heights, and the burglars shot a dog. Now, that's just awful!"

"But we don't know if it was them, do we Auntie?"

"They practically admitted it to Nard! Isn't that so, boy?"

"Kind of," I said.

"Time we told the sheriff," Anna said. "They might shoot a person next. Lord knows, it don't do any good to tell Mr. Robinson that his son has a gun and shoots it at things."

"Did you?" I asked her.

"Yes." It bothered her just to think about it. "He said it was a lie, that his precious boy would never do such a terrible thing. He might sneak onto the farm and do some little devilment, but he wouldn't go into a house and destroy things."

"How did he think your house got trashed?"

"He said the orphan boy who told me about it done it, then blamed someone else."

That's what Julie had thought, too. We pulled off the road and onto the driveway. The farmhouse was still a quarter of a mile away. "What if we found that other bullet?" I asked. "Would that convince him?"

"That's right!" Anna said. "There's a bullet somewhere!"

We looked all over the walls and ceiling for a hole, but couldn't find one. Then I stood where Erik had stood in the living room and aimed my hand around. It pointed at the couch! We swarmed all over it until Julie found a hole underneath a button in one of the cushions. Anna peeled off the fabric and a bullet was stuck in the stuffing.

"Are you going to show it to Mr. Robinson?" I asked. "Maybe you could sell it to him for twenty thousand dollars!"

"That wouldn't be right," Anna said, tossing the little chunk of lead up and down in her hand. "I'm goin' to take this to the sheriff. If those boys shot a dog, they belong in jail."

It didn't work out that way. When Anna gave the sheriff's department the bullet, she thought they might put *her* in jail. They asked her all kinds of questions, like why hadn't the incident been reported when it happened? Did she know the Robinsons? When they found out Mr. Robinson had lent her twenty thousand dollars, they didn't like it.

But when they compared the bullet with the one that hit the dog, they liked it better. Both were .38 calibre, whatever that meant. But the one in the dog had hit a bone or something, so they couldn't be sure the bullets were from the same weapon. "The long and short of it," Anna said, "is they need the gun."

Twenty-One

I hadn't seen my "servant" all week. I knew why. Vinci knew if I caught him, I'd kill him. He'd hidden my drawings, which left me nothing to show the man I'd talked to at Inventors Protection Agency. That creep-o hand wanted me to be like Leonardo da Vinci and live in poverty.

But Wednesday night after school, Anna and Farley had to meet with Farley's lawyer. They no sooner left than Vinci walked in! He got over by Julie, and I couldn't execute him in front of her...when I had an idea. Maybe I could get him to do a new set of drawings. I needed them anyway because the design of the flycycle had changed. I sat down at the kitchen table and drew stick figures with my right hand. This flycycle had a built-in gear that would drive the propeller, and a suprone harness. He fleshed them out to look like what I meant.

They were great. You could see how everything worked with the new design. The pilot would run down a slope, the way hang glider pilots do, until she was airborne. Then she'd swing her feet up and let the harness support her back. Her feet would be in perfect position to start pedaling, and the propeller would start turning, pulling her into the sky. Now was my chance. I reached for the drawings...

But my rotten "servant" grabbed them ahead of me! I'd forgotten he knows what I think. "Hey," I hollered at him. "Come back with those!" But he was gone.

"Why did he do that?" Julie asked.

"I don't know." I heard the door to her room slam. "He's playing hide-and-seek, or something. I'm going after him!"

"I'll go with you." But when she stood up, she made a face like she'd been stabbed. "Oh!" She staggered for the living room couch, grabbing at her back.

Pain tore away at Julie's face. I grabbed her by the arm to keep her from falling down. We got over to the couch, where she flopped on her stomach and gritted her teeth. I ran to her room, looking for Vinci.

He was there, standing on top of Julie's desk and writing a note. I was all conflicted out. I wanted to kill him, but that would have to wait until he'd fixed Julie's back. "Julie needs you," I said. "She's on the couch."

He slid off her desk and scooted out of there. I read the note.

*Be not angry with me, young Nard. I know you
better than you know yourself. At this time in your
life, you cannot be trusted with the fruits of your
imagination. Your mind has matured in some re-
spects, but not in virtue. Do not despair, for one day,
you will grow to the wondrous realization that there
is far greater reward in giving than in greed. Then
you will no longer need my controlling hand.*

*That time will come. And when it arrives, your true
nature will shine forth on this world, for all to see.*

The creep! What did he know? He'd never been an
orphan! I searched Julie's room for my drawings...and
saw Julie's diary in a desk drawer. I shouldn't have, but
I opened it up. It might tell me where she hid things.

*If only I could take it all back. I just wish and wish
and wish, but there isn't any way. Nard is the best
friend I've ever had in my life, and I said that awful
thing to him! He doesn't even know how smart he is,
or how much he means to Auntie, or my dad, or me.*

What the heck was that all about? What had Julie ever
said to me that was so terrible? I didn't like her calling me
smart either, or that other stuff. It made me suspicious.

*I wonder if he'll ever know how many times I've
died since then. I can still hear myself, and see his*

face, too. "You aren't in my family," I said. "We're not related." All he wanted was to be part of my family, but I wouldn't let him in. How could I ever have been so cruel?

He's given me hope. He and Vinci, that strange little hand, have given me a reason to live. I only pray that some day, somehow, I can give Nard as much as he's given me.

I slammed the diary shut and put it back where I'd found it.

I'm just an orphan, I thought. Who said my life had to get so complicated?

The next day was Thursday. The day after that, Julie would graduate from hang gliding school. Her back looked straight to me, so I knew Vinci had been compromising her.

The students had to glide to the ground from a cliff. Mack and I watched from the meadow below, where they'd land. "Isn't the CUTA! contest August 15?" he asked.

"Yes."

"That leaves you six weeks to build and test your flycycle. Will that be enough time?"

"Sure. Just change the fabric, and install a propeller and a drive shaft to the nose . . . hmmm." I hadn't thought about it, to tell the truth. "Clip on a wheel for a gear, attach it to the keel. My gosh." There was a lot to do. I didn't really care, except I did, sort of. Winning the contest would be fun.

We stopped to watch Julie take off in a training glider. She was way better than the others. "She's amazing," Mack said, smiling. "Sometimes I think she's too good." Julie was trying a suprone harness for the first time. She swung her feet over the "A" bar like she'd been doing it all her life and stretched her feet out in front of her as if she were on a swing.

"How could she be too good?"

"She needs to learn one step at a time, like everybody else. But she's got such a natural feeling for it that she can cut corners. She might not take the dangers seriously enough."

"Will you sell us the twenty-footer?"

"One's on its way. But she'll need another week of training before I'll sell it to her."

"How much will that cost?"

"Nothing." She'd sailed through the sky for half a mile, and we watched her slide out of the harness for her landing. "Some things I don't do for money."

Julie flared her wing a little crooked and stumbled some, but except for that, it was perfect. Mack clapped his hands and ran toward her. "Good for you, Julie! That was nice!"

I ran over, too. I'd never seen her so happy about any-thing. "Man is that cool!" she kind of shouted at us. "I *love* it, it's so cool!"

It sure looked like fun. Maybe some day I could fly with the right kind of prosthetic device, but I'd never be able to do it with just one hand. Still, watching her gave me a lift, for some reason. "Wait'll you're in my flycycle," I told her.

"Nard, we need to talk about that," Mack said.

He might want to talk about it, but *I* didn't. He'd bring up more complications. That's the big trouble with reali-ty, I thought—even though sometimes, complications are fun. I liked it when reality handed me a problem I could solve.

So I wanted to talk, too. Sort of. "Yeah, I know."

The students were outside, practicing running down hills without looking at the ground. Mack and I sat in his office. "Your ideas are extraordinary," he said, "but you won't be able to build it without help."

"Why can't I?"

"You need a machine shop, for starters. You'll never attach the propeller and all that hardware to the keel with-out the right tools." Farley's workbench in the barn didn't even come close. "Everything has to be done with preci-sion," Mack said. "The angle of the drive shaft through the nose has to be worked out exactly. The size of the propeller has to be figured out exactly. Computing the optimum lift to generate, the weights and balances, all kinds of technical and engineering detail. You can't do it from the seat of your pants."

Mack had a machine shop and a computer. "Could I use yours?"

"Get real, Nard. You don't have the experience. Where will you find a lightweight plastic hollow propeller, for example? How would you make one? Changing the fabric for the sail will also take an expertise you don't have. You won't know how to peel it off without damaging the frame, or how to fasten lighter fabric on so it'll stay."

Mack had the expertise. "Would you help me?"

"I'd love to, but I need to make a living." He took a deep breath, like just before diving into water. "But I'd be willing to go into business with you."

I gulped. What would that be like? "Who gets the prize money?" I blurted out. "Would I have to split it with you?"

He looked at me with surprise. "I don't care about the money from the contest."

"You don't?"

"Nard, if it works, I'd like to build them and sell them."

I thought of the millions of dollars I wanted for my life. "Then you'd make all the money off my invention," I said.

"Wait a minute. If we're in business together, we both make money."

"Who'd make the most?"

He took another deep breath to keep from getting mad. "Nard, inventions aren't worth anything if they don't work. Nobody will know if this one works until it gets built." He put his hand on my shoulder. "We'd have to trust each other to be fair. Believe me, I wouldn't cheat you. Life's too short for that."

I didn't know if I could trust him or not. I didn't know if he could trust me, either.

"Look. Let me help you build it," he said. "Then we'll know if it works. The money from the contest is yours, but we'd be partners after that. We'd build them and sell them."

"I'd be your partner?" I asked him. "Like, we'd split the money we made off of the flycycles?"

"You young guys." He took his hand off my shoulder and measured me with his eyes. "All you care about is money."

So I'm a greedy slug. But words from Julie's diary floated through my brain. "I've got like a family, Mack. Julie needs an operation, and Anna could lose her farm, and Julie's dad could go to prison for forty years. So yeah, I care about money."

"Nard?" Julie said.

She was standing behind me. I hadn't heard her come up. "Oh. Hi."

"You really want in my dumb family?"

"I don't know. I guess."

"Cool."

Twenty-Two

That night, Julie told Anna what I'd said to Mack. Anna gave me a big hug, which was all right, but Farley had to give me one, too. He smelled for one thing, and for another, it felt weird with them thinking I was a saint.

The next day, Mack and I made a deal. He'd help me build a flycycle out of the twenty-foot hang glider he'd ordered if he could manufacture them after the CUTA! contest. I'd get half the profits, which should be two hundred dollars for each one he sold! We shook hands on it.

I still thought about the guy at Inventors Protection Agency, though. What if he said I could do better?

Things moved fast as the contest got closer. The faster they moved, the better for Julie's back. I knew without asking that Vinci compromised her every morning, before Anna or Farley drove us to the hang gliding school.

We were in a routine at Air Adventures. Mack taught classes and worked with Julie at the same time. She learned more and more about hang gliding, while I explored the equipment in his machine shop, learning how to operate some of it.

When the twenty-foot glider arrived from the manufacturer, I helped Mack assemble it while Julie worked with his students. Teaching others the basics would teach her, Mack said, and everybody learned when Julie flew the new bird.

A couple of times, she caught a thermal lift that took her way high into the sky. Mack was relieved when he saw how cautiously she responded to the risk and the thrill. She didn't go crazy and ride the glider out of sight, but rode out the thermal, then looped around and landed.

Watching her in the sky loaded my brain with ideas. Could the wing be filled with hot air, like a balloon? Could the drive shaft be made to swivel where it went through the keel? Then Julie could aim the propeller up, down, left, or right, with her feet. A tail rudder and ailerons would make it even more maneuverable. She could operate them with grip controls, like ones on a mountain bike.

At night I'd go to my room with Julie, and we'd talk while I drew stick figures. My "servant" always showed up and did great sketches, which he'd hide after letting me see them. I really needed them to show Mack so he could work out the engineering. But Vinci didn't trust me... Until one morning, all the drawings were on top of my desk in a stack! There was a note on top, naturally.

> *Young master. You have made much progress in your journey toward virtue. The time has come when you must sail your own ship. Permit me to offer one final bit of advice. Remember those who love you, and allow your conscience to be your guide.*
>
> *May God be with you.*
>
> *Your obedient servant, known to you as "Vinci."*

It made me mad. Why did everything have to be like a lesson in morality? Well, I'd been an orphan for thirteen years and already knew some things. When opportunity knocks, take advantage of it, because you may never get another chance.

I grabbed the drawings, stuffed them into an envelope, and snuck into the kitchen where I boosted ten dollars out of the cash jar. Nobody saw me leave. When the six A.M. bus left Bergen Lake Road that morning for Eldorado, I was on it.

It had been months since I'd been in downtown Eldorado. I wandered around until eight-thirty, checking out luxury cars and drooling over the displays in the shopping malls. There sure is a lot to buy for people with money.

The office for Inventors Protection Agency was in a small building where the pawn shops are and the bums hang out. I thought I might see somebody I knew. At nine o'clock, I stood in front of a frosted glass door that had the name of the business painted on it, and knocked.

"Come in!" a man's voice hollered.

I walked into a small room. Cardboard boxes stuffed with models, papers, and books lined the walls. A man with long gray hair in a ponytail, wearing a Colorado Rockies hat backwards, stood up. He'd been sitting behind a battered wooden desk. "You're not selling anything, are you?"

"No sir. I called you up about a flycycle? You said get down here with the idea?"

He nodded and sat down. "Lemme see what you've got," he said, sticking out his hand.

I gave him the drawings. There wasn't anything to sit on, so I just stood there and watched. His eyes opened wide as he looked at them. "I don't know," he said. "Tell you what. I'll make a copy of these." He jumped up and trotted out of the room.

It made me nervous, but he came back a few minutes later and shut the door. "Wouldn't you know, the copy machine broke down," he said. "I'll just keep these and we'll be in touch. What's your number?" He sat down behind his desk and held a pencil over a pad.

"I want my drawings back."

"What?" He sounded like he hadn't heard me right.

"I want my drawings back."

"You don't trust me? You think I'm a thief?" He smiled, stood up, then threw the drawings at me! They scattered all over the floor. "Get out'a here, punk," he said. "I never want to see you again."

It took me thirty seconds to pick them up. He loomed over me like a giant the whole time. I ran out the door.

What got into the guy? I wondered, later, at a donut shop. I had a few donuts and tried to decide what to do. Finally I thought of a lie I could tell Anna and called her up.

"Nard honey, where are you?" she asked. "Everybody's worried sick!"

She never made it easy to lie. "I had to come to town and didn't want to bother you over it," I said. "A friend of mine got in trouble, and he called me up and—"

"Honey, if he's a friend of yours, he's a friend of all of us. You just bring him out to the farm. Set right where you are and I'll come get you."

"Don't do that," I said. "I mean, he's okay now. We talked and I lent him five dollars from the cash jar." I waited for her to explode. "I took ten dollars," I told her.

"I know," she said. "You forgot to put an IOU in there, but I just figured it was an emergency."

Is that all the heck I'd get? I deserved more than that. "Is Julie there?" I'd started to snuffle and to feel really guilty and rotten.

"Yep. She wants to talk to you."

"Nard? Are you okay?" Julie asked. "Mack is out of his mind. Even Daddy was worried. Me too, a little." She laughed. "Where are you?"

"Downtown."

"Tell me where and we'll come get you."

"You go out to Mack's," I said. "I'll take the bus, which won't take long."

She could hear me snuffling. "You okay?"

"Yeah."

"Okay, see you in a while." She hung up.

I'd made a huge mistake. That guy tried to steal my invention. I stared out the window of the bus that would take me to Mack's, watching the city traffic thin out and the trees slide by. Lucky for me his copy machine didn't work, I thought, going through the drawings to make sure I'd gotten all of them . . .

They weren't the same! My gosh. These were copies! He'd kept the originals!

It was ten o'clock when I got off the bus at Air Adventures, but so much had happened that it felt a lot later. There was no way I could tell anyone what the guy at Inventors Protection Agency had done. I was stuck with my lies. Probably nothing would come of them, I hoped, walking into the hangar.

Julie saw me first. "Nard!" she yelled, running toward me. "Mack! Nard's here!"

He was happy to see me, too. What if he knew the truth?

When I gave the copies of the drawings to Mack, his mouth opened with surprise. "Did you do these?" he asked. I shrugged, not knowing what to say. "They're brilliant," he said. He couldn't take his eyes off of them. "Like sketches from the notebooks of Leonardo da Vinci. It's as though they were drawn by his hand."

Julie looked at me kind of strange, then pounded her forehead with her hand. "I just thought of the perfect name!"

"For what?" I asked.

"The flycycle. *Leonardo's Hand!*"

"I like it," Mack said.

I wasn't enthusiastic, to tell the truth. It could give my "servant" an ego problem. But I didn't say anything because Mack put his arm over my shoulders. "You know what, partner?" he said to me. "That flycycle of yours is going to fly!"

Twenty-Three

A few nights later, during dinner, Anna told me that Polly Chan, the television anchorperson on Channel Nine, had called that day and wanted to talk to me. "Why?" I asked Anna. "What about?"

"Your entry in CUTA!, boy. Channel Nine is doing a newscast about it." She looked at the clock on the wall. "It starts in ten minutes."

"My entry?" I didn't get it. "I thought you entered it. You paid for it didn't you?"

She put her hand on my arm. "It's your ideas that we're ridin' on the coattails of. I entered it in your name. You're the one who deserves the credit, and all of us know that."

She sounded proud of me, which made the cornbread

hard to eat, because I wasn't very proud of myself. But I got it down in plenty of time, along with two legs of chicken, a gallon of milk, and half a pound of mashed potatoes. We all trooped into the living room and turned on the TV.

A minute or so later, the screen showed Polly Chan standing on Table Mountain. "Eighteen days from now, a handful of hopefuls will try to breathe life into the ancient dream of humankind," she said. "In the last hundred years, we've conquered the sky with airplanes and engines. But will we ever fly on our own, like birds?" The wind blew her hair around like a movie star's when a serious-looking old guy with a gray moustache and glasses walked into the picture. "This is Garrison Ford," she said to the camera. "How are you, sir?"

"Fine," he said, standing next to her. "Wonderful. Mr. Turner sends his apologies."

"That's Glen Turner, the billionaire sponsor of CUTA!?" she asked.

"He's a bit camera-shy and never appears in public."

"But he isn't backing out, is he?" Polly Chan asked. "The contest is still on?"

"Indeed it is."

"In spite of the fact that there are so few contestants?"

"That's right." When he faced the camera, it felt like he was talking to me. "Mr. Turner is a great believer in the inventive genius of the American people," he said. "We at CUTA! thought a hundred thousand dollars would attract entries from all over the world, but it didn't quite work out that way."

"What happened, sir?"

"We're hearing two things. The first is that the rules are too restrictive," he said. "Several college programs have told us it's impossible for them to enter something that might work with a spending limit of $4,000, especially on such short notice. Secondly, some aeronautical engineers are telling us it's impossible anyway. A twenty-foot wingspan limit, at this elevation, simply won't work." He shrugged.

"How many entries are there?" she asked.

"Only three contestants qualified."

"Not quite the Super Bowl for Eldorado, is it?" Polly Chan said.

"No, but there should still be lots of excitement. And who knows? One of them might actually do it."

"The prize money is one hundred thousand dollars. How can it be won?"

"By flying northeast from where we're standing to Greeley Lake. Then south to Eldorado Park, then back here. A distance of thirty-seven miles." He smiled. "There may not be a winner this year, to be honest. The money would then be invested, giving us a bigger pot next year."

Polly Chan looked into the camera. "So there you have it, folks. The CUTA! contest hasn't been canceled, but the expectations have certainly been scaled down. Nevertheless, we'll be here on August 15 to see what happens." She started walking off again, letting the wind blow her hair. "Our newscast will begin at nine in the morning. Won't you join us?" The screen faded into a commercial.

"Shut that dang thing off, Farley!" Anna said. "Thirty-seven miles! I'd forgotten about that part."

Maybe Julie had too. She didn't look very confident.

The week before the contest, the flycycle was ready to be tested. Mack canceled school that day, and Anna and Farley were there to watch.

Julie carried *Leonardo's Hand* out of the hangar like a monster feather. It only weighed twenty-eight pounds.

What a cool-looking bird. Anna and Farley stared at her. "Can Julie fly that thing?" Anna asked. The fabric was the color of the sky, with a picture of Leonardo da Vinci's flying machine stenciled in red on the wings. The words *Leonardo's Hand* were on there too, in glowing gold. "It looks like a big moth."

A rudder stuck up above the end of the keel. A control lever would turn it right or left. We'd mounted a small wing back there too, with a control lever to roll it up or down. The propeller, at the front of the drive shaft, angled up ten degrees through the nose. Julie could swing it back and forth or up or down with her feet, which locked onto the pedals of the big gear she would pump. It hung like a bicycle wheel from a spot near the front of the keel.

There were goosebumps all over my body when I

watched Julie walk to the top of the hill. She held the bird by the control bar and let the breeze help with the weight. She knew just when to lean this way or that way so it wouldn't catch the wing like a kite and blow her away.

She turned into the wind at the top of the hill. Man, it was exciting. I felt something tug at my pants cuff.

Vinci! He'd been hiding from me. I hadn't seen him for days. I didn't want him to know it, but I was kind of glad to see him again. When no one was looking, I reached down and let him crawl up my arm. He got in my hat.

Julie trotted down the hill, keeping the wing at a low attitude while she built up speed. She looked like pictures I'd seen of the goddess Diana, chasing a deer. Twenty yards later, the wing lifted her off the ground . . .

She was flying! She swung her feet into position and the propeller started grinding away! It pulled her up and into the air until she was fifty feet off the ground!

"Level her out!" Mack yelled, and the bird leveled out. "Ease her into a turn!" The bird banked gently to the right, heading south. "Okay, now turn her the other way!" Julie did, flying over our heads.

I cheered, making more noise than I'd ever made in my life. I couldn't help myself. Even Vinci squeaked a little.

"How do you feel?" Mack called.

She looked at him through the goggles under her helmet and gave him a "thumbs up."

"Great! Put her down!"

Julie wiggled the wings, enough for a sign, then looped slowly into the wind. She landed exactly where she'd taken off.

Tears leaked out of Anna and Farley's eyes. Julie's knees were shaking, and Mack got a grip on the bird. "It works!" she said. "I can really fly it, Nard. It works!"

"What's that thing on your head?" Mack asked me. "It looks like..." A small gust of wind yanked him backwards, and Vinci stuffed himself into my pants pocket.

"I didn't see anything!" Julie said, yanking off her helmet.

Then she sat down on the ground and cried.

Twenty-Four

The CUTA! contest would start in an hour and a half. Mack drove Julie and me to the top of Table Mountain.

The mesa looked like a giant butcher's block from a distance. A road had been carved out of one side like a long ramp for wheelchairs.

On top, it was big, flat, and empty, like a chunk of Kansas prairie. A hundred soccer fields would fit up there with room to spare. *Leonardo's Hand* had her wings folded and was wrapped in canvas. She'd been lashed to a carrier on top of Mack's car and looked like a long thin rocket.

"Where are all the people?" Julie asked. "This doesn't look like the Super Bowl to me."

"It doesn't start until ten," Mack said.

"What am I supposed to do until then?" she asked nervously. "My hands are sweating. Can somebody stop my hands from sweating?"

"Relax," Mack said. "Don't worry about it."

"Easy for you to say. I should have stayed in bed. Where are Auntie and my dad? I don't see them."

"They're coming later," I said.

"They'd better. I need all the moral support I can get. At least my back feels good. But is . . . ?" She looked at me. "Did you bring it? I mean, I could have but I've been so busy thinking about all the things that could go wrong."

I didn't know whether she meant Vinci or the unicycle. She wanted the unicycle to ride around on and get loose before the contest started, and my "servant" for comfort. He still belonged to me he said, but I knew he liked Julie better. "It's in the trunk," I said, meaning the unicycle.

"What about . . . ?"

"Up top, with the flycycle."

A crowd-control cop told us to park near the starting line, which had been marked off like the goal line on a football field. Flat grass-covered ground stretched out in all directions for half a mile.

When we parked, Mack and I got out. Julie stayed inside and turned on the radio. "This won't be easy," Mack said, looking around.

It looked easy to me. The weather was perfect. There wasn't a cloud in the sky. "What's wrong?" I asked.

"No wind today. No hill for Julie to run down. How will she get enough lift to get airborne?"

Good question. "Jump off a cliff?"

"Not allowed. The rules say they have to be flying within two hundred yards of the starting line."

"What will we do?"

"Pray for wind. I don't know."

He lifted the flycycle off the top of the car and stuck it on the ground. Vinci was under the canvas, and I got near him. When no one was watching, he crawled up my leg and jumped into the back pouch of the bicycle shirt I'd worn that day. I felt like a genetically altered kangaroo, with the pouch on backwards.

There's more to assembling a hang glider than meets the eye, and flycycles are more complicated than hang gliders. We attached the control bar to the keel and stood her up. She looked like a dragonfly with folded wings. We spread out the leading edges, inserted the battens, raised the kingpin and secured the lines. I'd wait as long as possible before inflating the wings with hot air. It took both of us to get the drive shaft through the nose, lock in the propeller, and position the wheel that was really a big gear.

By the time she was close to ready, a crowd of people had gathered around. Mack was checking the rudder controls when Polly Chan showed up.

Polly Chan! We'd be famous! She stuck a microphone

in Mack's face. Her cameraman wore a headset and dark glasses. He aimed the camera at Mack like a bazooka, then pulled the trigger.

Did that mean we were on the air?

"Congratulations," Polly Chan said to Mack. "You're still in the race." She smiled.

"Miss, you're in the way," Mack said.

"It's a hang glider, isn't it?" she asked. "With a propeller? I like its simplicity."

"Please," Mack said, running his fingers along the line, checking for kinks. "Later."

"I'm from Channel Nine," Polly Chan said. "We're reporting this event, sir. It's a public event and I'd like to talk to you for a moment, Mr. Smith."

"That's him over there," Mack said, pointing at me.

"The young man? But the entry is in the name of Leonard Smith. Isn't that you?"

"No. He's the inventor."

One second later, the microphone was in my face and the camera was aimed at me. "Mr. Smith, is it? How old are you?"

"Thirteen."

"I'm amazed that someone so young could design this! What do you call it?"

"It's a flycycle." My gosh. I wondered how many people in the world were watching me.

"And you're the inventor? Really?"

I started to say "yes" when a man pushed his way through the crowd. He had long gray hair, tied in a bun behind his head, and looked like an artist. "That kid is a liar!" he shouted. It was the guy from Inventors Protection Agency! "*I'm* the inventor. He stole the invention from me!"

It felt like an elephant had stepped on my chest. I could feel the camera on me and knew I looked like a crook. Polly Chan went right on talking, like a reporter watching a war. "Let me set the stage," she said to TV-land. "We're on top of Table Mountain, a large flat mountain near Eldorado. The CUTA! contest will begin in"—she looked at her watch— "half an hour. A hundred entrants from all over the world had been predicted, but the field is very small. It's down to three."

She looked up into the sky and the cameraman panned around while she talked. "It's incredibly beautiful up here. The air is fresh, there are no clouds in an incredibly blue sky, and now we are caught in an unfolding drama. Here is a flying machine"—the cameraman pointed at *Leonardo's Hand*— "that just might fool all the experts. It's a uniquely simple flying bicycle design with a lot of promise."

"It's a Flycycle!" the guy from Inventors Protection Agency shouted. "I copyrighted the name. You gotta pay me to use it!"

Polly Chan smiled, kind of with glee. "The inventor of

this so-called flycycle, according to the entry form, is this young man." The camera caught me gulping in terror. "However, this man"—she stuck the microphone in his face— "says he's the inventor. What is your name, sir?"

The camera turned to him. "Aaron Slade. That kid stole it from me and I can prove it! He snuck in my office and made copies of my drawings! Here. Look at these." He whipped out the drawings I'd showed him! "These are my original sketches. Look at his application. It's copies of my sketches!" His chin went out angrily, aimed right at me. "My lawyer is on his way, but I need to stop this fraud before I lose my rights!"

Julie and Mack stood by the car like statues that couldn't move. Polly Chan turned to me and so did the camera. "What do you have to say for yourself, Leonard Smith? Can you prove it's your invention?"

"I . . . well, see . . ." My mouth was like stuck in cement. It wouldn't move.

"We're waiting," Polly Chan said. "Can you explain?"

All I could do was clear my throat a few times.

"Miss Chan," Mack said. He walked in front of her. "I don't know how this man got our drawings, but I know Leonard Smith has a patent pending on this invention."

"I do?" I asked.

"I know because I got it for him," Mack said. "He and I are partners."

"You did?" I squeaked, like a little mouse.

"Thieves!" Aaron Slade hollered. "A pair of thieves! You'll *both* hear from my lawyers!"

"I think we should settle this," Polly Chan said, "without lawyers. Does anyone here want to bring in lawyers?" she asked all the people standing around.

"No!" "Boo!" "Let's not do *that!*"

"Mr. Slade," Polly Chan said, "draw something for me. Prove to me and everyone here that you did these sketches. And Mr. Smith, you do the same."

"Great idea!" Slade said. "But I'd need a sketchpad, pencils, an easel."

"We'll get them for you," Polly Chan said. "It's time for a commercial break. Please, all of you watching, stay with us." She smiled at the camera. "And now back to the studio."

When the camera was off, she changed. "One of you is a fraud," she said to Slade and me. "I'm going to find out who it is and film it. Won't that be fun?"

I wanted to run for the edge of the mountain and jump off. Instead, Mack helped me to the car. "You okay?" he asked, his arm over my shoulder.

"No," I said. "I'm a cheater and a liar and a jerk. I didn't trust you."

"Did you steal those drawings from Aaron Slade?"

"No! He stole them from me. See..." My mouth filled up with cement again.

"I know Slade," Mack said. "He's stolen inventions from friends of mine and will do anything for money. How did you get tangled up with him?"

"I...I thought I could get a better deal."

Mack glared at me. "Some partner *you* are," he said.

"I screwed up. Can we..."

"Look at me." I did. He put his hands on my shoulders and stared through my eyes into my brain. About a minute later, he winked and pulled me toward him. "It's not easy being thirteen and as smart as you." He gave me a hug, then let go. "But from now on, we're up front with each other. Right?"

"We're still partners?" I asked him.

"As far as I'm concerned, we are." Then a funny expression came over his face. "Don't look now," he said, "but here comes Polly Chan. She's got a sketchpad for you."

"Mr. Smith?" she said to me. Her expression was way bad, even though she smiled. "Are you ready for this?"

Twenty-Five

How could I prove to Polly Chan I'd done the sketches? I hadn't! All I can draw are stick figures! "Here you are," she said to me, handing me a sketchpad and some pencils. "Mind if we watch your work?" Her cameraman had me in his sights.

"Yes, he minds!" Julie said, walking into the picture.

"Who are you?" Polly Chan asked as the camera focused on her.

"Julie Marne. I'm on the team. I'm the pilot."

"Can you actually fly this, what do you call it?"

"A flycycle," Julie said. "Its name is *Leonardo's Hand*. And he invented it." She pointed at me.

"Where did the name *Leonardo's Hand* come from?" Chan asked. "Is there a story behind that?"

"Leonardo da Vinci and Leonard Smith are related," Julie said, then blushed. "Like they're spiritually related." That sounded pretty far out. I wondered what she would say next. "They're both inventors with cool ideas about flying, so we named it after his hand."

"Yes, but why?"

"If you look at the sketches, you'll see," Julie said. "You can't tell them apart. The ones Nard does are just like the ones Leonardo da Vinci did five hundred years ago."

"Really!" Polly Chan said. "Amazing, if true. Mr. Smith, why don't you..."

"He can't," Julie said. "Not with people watching. He's very sensitive and gets all flustered. Isn't that right, Nard?"

I couldn't talk. All I could do was nod my head.

"How can he prove his case then?" Polly Chan asked. "Should all these people just take his word for it?" She waved at the crowd of people, but her wave seemed to include the whole world.

"You won't need to do that," Julie said. "Come on, Nard." She took the sketchpad and pencils away from me, then grabbed my hand. "We're going to the car," she said to Polly Chan. "You have to promise you'll leave us alone for five minutes. He'll draw something and you'll see. Okay?"

"But what if there are drawings in the car? How will we know they weren't drawn before?"

My mouth unlocked. "It'll be a new idea," I stammered. "Something we need for the contest. See, Julie can't fly from here. She needs a hill to run down for lift, to get off the ground. But there's a way to do it without a hill."

"Well!" Polly Chan declared. "What's this new and brilliant insight of yours?"

"I'll draw it. As soon as you leave me and Julie alone." I looked at Mack who had his hand on his chin, thinking.

Polly Chan shrugged her shoulders. "The plot thickens, it appears. Five minutes?" I gulped and nodded. "Go ahead," she said, then walked toward Aaron Slade, dragging the cameraman with her. Slade was slashing away at his easel. "In the meantime, we'll follow the progress of Mr. Slade."

Julie pulled me toward Mack's car and tried to open the door, but it was locked. "Hey Mack," she said. "Open it up."

He pulled an electronic key out of his pocket and punched the button. "What's going on, guys?" he asked. "Am I in on this, partner?"

"I . . . well . . . no. You've got to trust me."

He laughed, kind of a skeptical laugh. "The door's open," he told us, walking away.

Julie and I climbed into the back seat of Mack's car. "Is anyone watching?" I asked, before dragging out Vinci.

"I don't think so," Julie said. "But you never know when we'll be back on television."

We closed the door and windows and huddled down so no one could see. I'd been carrying my "servant" in the pouch of my bike shirt, and he crawled out and got on the floor. "Hi, Vinci," Julie said to him. "Didn't I tell you?" she said to me.

"Tell me what?"

"Girls are better liars than boys."

That broke us both up.

"What's your new idea?" she asked. "It better be good. There's no wind and no hill. How will I get airborne? I can't run fast enough."

"You won't have to if this works." I drew a stick figure and showed it to Vinci. "Back to square one. The problem is you've never practiced it."

Julie watched him flesh my idea out on the sketch-pad. "That's so cool, Nard," she said. "Why didn't I think of that?"

We heard a knock on the window and looked up. Polly Chan's grinning face stared at me. "Time's up!" I heard her say.

"Just a minute!" Julie yelled at her. Vinci was writing a note:

My splendid young friends:

I shall remain here, hidden from the prying eyes of the world. Through the thoughts of my young master, I shall follow the progess of the apparatus you have named for me. You have done me much honor, for which please accept my humble thanks.

The future is not mine to know. But of this much, there can be no doubt. Young Julie, you are indeed a champion and will remain one, no matter what the day's events bring. Young "Nard," as you insist, you are also a champion. In truth, my sense is that the world is filled with young champions, and I no longer am in despair.

Now go. And may God be with you.

As Julie and I read it, he slid under the front seat of the car. "Thank you," Julie said to him.

I felt better, too. I didn't want to hug him, but I didn't want to flatten him, either. Julie and I got out of the car and locked it, and I gave Polly Chan the sketchbook with the sketches my servant Vinci had drawn.

When she looked at them, she laughed. "You're kidding me," she said. "No one can do that."

"Julie can," I told her.

"I'll say this much, Mr. Smith. Your drawings appear, to me at any rate, to have been drawn by whoever drew these." She held up the ones Aaron Slade had stolen from me.

"Give me those!" Slade said, grabbing them out of her hand. "The kid's a gifted forger, a con man! But *I* drew these. It's just for some reason, I can't draw today. Haven't had an idea for a week or two, and I'm out of practice."

"Those are mine!" I yelled at him. "You stole them from me that day I went to see you!"

Slade tried to walk off with them, but Mack stood in his way. "You're aren't going anywhere with those sketches, Slade," he said. "*You* didn't draw them. You can't draw like that."

"Out'a my way!"

But the crowd surrounded him too. He couldn't move.

"Isn't this fun, everyone?" Polly Chan asked. The cameraman was shooting the whole scene. "Mr. Slade, why not leave them with me? I'm a disinterested person who obviously can't steal them from either of you, not with thousands of people as witnesses." She held out her hand for them.

Slade had no choice and gave them to her. "You're all gonna get it from my lawyer!" he grumped, stalking off.

Twenty-Six

A large grassy plain, the size of five soccer fields laid out end to end, was roped off from the crowd of people. A smooth paved runway, five hundred yards long, stretched through the middle from west to east. The starting line was at the west end of the runway, and the rules said the flying machines had to be airborne before reaching a marker two hundred yards from the starting line. The crowd stood behind a rope barricade that wrapped around the takeoff point.

The other flying machines and crews waited for us at the starting line. Mack carried *Leonardo's Hand* over his head and I walked next to him. Julie rode around the runway on her unicycle, warming up and stretching her legs. The butterflies in my stomach were intense.

A little old lady and a monster crowded to the front of the rope barricade near the starting line. They waved and yelled at us. "Daddy!" Julie hollered, pedaling over to them. "Auntie! You made it!" They hugged and kissed, then Julie went back into her warm-up routine.

A breeze started from the west. "That won't help," Mack said. "It's from the wrong direction. This could be a real disaster."

He'd seen the latest sketch and knew what my idea was. "I like that breeze," I said. "Julie can use it."

"How?"

"The rules say she has to be in the air between the starting line and that two hundred yard marker, but they don't say she has to start at the starting line. If she starts at the marker instead, she can take off into the wind."

He grinned at me. "You're right."

"Ladies and gentlemen, the contest is about to begin," a voice blared over a loudspeaker. "For safety reasons, the contestants will take off one at a time." Mack and I got *Leonardo's Hand* in line behind the other two flying machines and Julie pedaled over to us. "Our first entry is called *Tri-Winged Flyer* and the pilot is Teddy Frantz. Teddy is a professional bicycle racer and tells us he's used to flying, although usually much lower to the ground."

The *Tri-Winged Flyer* had three levels of wings stacked on top of each other. The bottom wing was four feet off the ground. Three struts angled out from the undercarriage like a tripod with small wheels attached to them. The pilot sat in a cockpit carved out of the middle wing.

"Are you ready, Teddy?" the announcer called out.

Teddy was built like a frog, with huge leg muscles and skinny arms. He put his helmet on, locked his feet into expensive racing bicycle pedals, then stuck his thumb in the air.

"All right, go!"

Teddy pumped himself up with deep breaths. Then he started pedaling, slowly at first, but building up speed. As his legs churned away a big propeller behind him started to spin, pushing him forward.

Man, he was strong! The propeller turned into a blur and the *Tri-Winged Flyer* built up speed. Twenty yards, fifty yards, then a hundred, and still moving faster. Everybody there, including me, cheered him on!

He only had ten yards to go when it started inching its way off the ground! "Go! Go!" everybody hollered. "You're off!" The wheels touched just in front of the marker, then the *Tri-Winged Flyer* started climbing into the air! From a distance, it looked like a tall sail!

Julie looked worried, watching him fly off Table Mountain. "What chance do I have against Teddy Frantz?"

"He's got a long way to go," Mack said. "He won't be able to rest."

"Neither will I!"

"Yes, you will. There should be a thermal when you get over the edge of the mesa. Take it. Get some lift. You'll find others on the way around the course, so you'll be able to get some altitude and glide."

"How is that for excitement?" the loudspeaker blared. "Now we know how the Wright brothers felt. We have ground spotters with TV coverage all along the route, so you'll be able to watch history in the making today."

Mack set the flycycle down, angling it so the breeze wouldn't blow it over. "Am I next?" Julie asked, her voice cracking with nervousness.

"I don't think so," Mack said.

"Mr. Spyro," the loudspeaker shouted. "How are you doing?"

The other flying machine was a hang glider on top of what looked like a pogo stick. It had a large overhead propeller like on a helicopter. An older man held it up for the younger man, who sat on a bicycle seat, pumping away. But the pumping didn't do anything. It didn't even budge the propeller. He'd been pumping for a long time too and it seemed to be getting harder and harder. Veins were popping out on his forehead and his legs had slowed down. "Gettin' there!" he yelled back.

"The next entry is called *Spyro's Gyro*," the announcer said. "Also human-powered of course, but the father and son team of Spyro and Spyro found a loophole in the rules. Chris, the son, is the pilot and he's literally been winding it up. Are any of you old enough to remember wind-up toys with rubber bands?"

"My gosh," I said to Mack. "Could he put enough energy in there to fly thirty-seven miles?"

Mack shrugged. He didn't look worried.

Chris got off the bicycle seat and shook his legs, while his dad held *Spyro's Gyro*. Chris put on a helmet and a minute later, sat down again on the seat.

"Is the team of Spyro and Spyro ready?" the announcer asked.

"Yes!"

"All right then. Go!"

It *was* a big pogo stick. Chris tilted forward, then started hopping down the runway. He could control the speed of the big propeller and let it spin slowly, lifting him up. At five feet above the ground, Chris took a monster hop and let the propellor spin faster!

He was in the air! He had a control bar, which he pulled back, angling his bird forward and letting the propeller spin some more! Everybody cheered! He was off!

We watched him clear the edge of Table Mountain. He was pumping again, winding his bird back up.

Could Julie beat him? I wondered, watching him glide away.

"Our final contestant is a trim looking ship indeed," the loudspeaker blared. "It's called *Leonardo's Hand*, and the pilot is thirteen-year-old Julie Marne. Julie, are you ready?"

"No!" she yelled.

"How much time do you need?"

Mack had buckled her into the harness that clipped her to the keel. We helped her balance the flycycle over her head, only this time, she wouldn't run down a hill into a wind. There was no hill and the wind was from the wrong direction. Somehow we had to get the unicycle under her. Julie would have to ride it while holding the bird over her head. It was her only chance to build up enough speed to get airborne.

"Thirty seconds!" she yelled. She sure looked tiny under that twenty-foot wing.

With Mack and me holding her, she sat on the unicycle and dropped her feet on the pedals. "Do you know what to do?" I asked her.

"I know what I'm *supposed* to do. The hard part will be doing it."

"I'm not worried about that," I told her. "Like my servant said, you're a champion."

"Your servant?" Mack asked.

"Just a joke between Nard and me," she told him.

"...Nine! Eight! Seven!" the loudspeaker blared.

"Do you want a push?" I asked.

"Just a little one."

"...Three! Two! One! Blast off, *Leonardo's Hand!*"

Julie teetered down the runway, pedaling slowly, getting the feel of riding the unicycle while balancing the flycycle over her head. She looked like a daredevil on a high wire over the Grand Canyon. The crowd moaned and gasped, hoping she'd stay up but expecting her to crash. She wobbled, then picked up enough speed to straighten out.

"Julie, you have to be in the air before you get to the marker," the announcer called. "Those are the rules."

"I will be!" she yelled.

At a hundred and fifty yards out, she got way over to one edge of the runway and leaned into a big U-turn.

"Are you coming back?" the announcer asked. "For another try at it?"

"No!" Julie yelled. "Here I go!"

Julie headed west, into the wind. It blew at four miles an hour. "Will it be enough?" I asked Mack.

"We'll see."

She leaned forward and cranked, building up speed, until she charged the starting line like a stampede. "Hey!" the announcer called. "What are you doing? Look out everyone!"

At fifty yards from the starting line, the flycycle started to climb! It lifted her off the unicycle just as I knew it would! The wheel with no one on it rolled a few feet, then fell over.

But nobody watched the unicycle. All eyes were on

Julie, who swung her feet through the control bar and locked them into the pedals of the big gear that drove the propeller. She pedaled hard and angry, determined to stay in the air. The propeller began to spin, but the bird slowed and dipped toward the runway. "Go!" Mack and I yelled. "You can do it!" The propeller spun faster and faster until the bird leveled out and started to climb!

A big cheer blew off the top of Table Mountain like an eruption. Julie was twenty feet off the ground and climbing into the breeze when she flew over the heads of the crowd. At an altitude of fifty feet above the ground, she banked around and headed east for Greeley Lake.

Twenty-Seven

When Julie flew off Table Mountain in *Leonardo's Hand*, Anna and Farley were so excited that they jumped into their truck and drove off to track her around the course. Hundreds of cars did the same thing. Mack and I stayed on the mesa in a tent set up by the race officials. The crews for the contestants were supposed to wait there and watch the race on TV.

It was crowded in the tent, with people milling around, stirring up dust. Four big-screen TVs hung from poles twelve feet off the ground. We found a place to stand, when I remembered Vinci. He should be here too. "Can I borrow the key to your car?" I asked Mack. "I forgot something."

"What?" he asked, fishing in his pocket and handing

it to me. I didn't know what to say, which showed on my face. "Hurry back," he said.

I ran for the car, opened the door, and saw Vinci on the back seat. "Julie's on her way to Greeley Lake," I told him. "It's on TV."

He seemed to know, and did a small nod. I put him in the pouch of my bicycle shirt. To make sure no one would see him, I laid a small repair kit on top of him. It had wire, pliers, and alan keys in a sack.

"You can't go in," a guard told me at the entrance to the tent. "It's reserved for..."

"Mr. Smith!" a man's deep voice said to the guard. "This is Leonard Smith, the inventor of *Leonardo's Hand*." I looked around, but didn't see the speaker. "Come in, sir!"

The guard stepped back to let me in. I tried to find the person who knew who I was but didn't see anyone, when a little guy at least a foot shorter than I was tapped me on the arm. I looked down.

"Mr. Smith." He had a face like a full moon that beamed with happiness. "Allow me to introduce myself. Glen Turner."

Glen Turner, the billionaire? "My gosh," I said, and gulped. "I didn't know you were—" Wrong thing to say I knew. After it was too late.

"A dwarf?" He boomed with laughter. "Yet I could have guessed that you have only one hand."

"Really? How come?"

"Because of your consummate cleverness, Mr. Smith. Those of us with physical obstacles to overcome must resort to cleverness and strategy to realize our desires. The average person has no need to resort to such tactics. You obviously have dug deeply within yourself to arrive at your flycycle design."

All the other conversations in the tent stopped. It was like he and I were alone. "Thanks," I said, not exactly sure of what he'd said.

"Are your parents here? They must be very proud of you."

"I don't have any. I'm an orphan."

"Well! Twice afflicted!" He beamed some more and handed me a card that had his name on it. "Please call me, young man. Perhaps one day we can do business."

Glen Turner, the billionaire, wanted to do business with me? My mouth opened as I watched him walk away.

Where had Mack gone I wondered, when I saw him watching one of the screens. It showed Julie! "This is an incredible sight," the TV announcer said. "We have all three of the contestants in view, although I'm not sure... Yes!" The screen showed all of them at the same time, like tropical fish in an aquarium. "That's *Spyro's Gyro*, gliding rapidly downward between *Leonardo's Hand* above, and the *Tri-Winged Flyer*, which is hugging the ground. Chris Spyro in the *Gyro* is trying desperately to wind his flyer up in those dives, but they seem to be getting lower and lower. Isn't that a sight!"

"Hello, Mr. Smith," a woman with a friendly face said to me. "Isn't this exciting?"

"Oh. Yeah." I tried to get over by Mack, but she stood in the way.

"I'm Patricia Truesdale." She held out her hand for me to shake.

"Hi."

"I just happened to hear you talking with Mr. Turner. You know who he is?"

"Sure. The billionaire."

"How old are you, Leonard? Fourteen? Fifteen?"

"Thirteen." I blushed.

"And you have no parents." Her face wrinkled with sadness. "I'm very concerned about you."

"You are? Why?"

A big man started toward us kind of like a battleship in the ocean. Ms. Truesdale put a hand on my shoulder and pulled me around so I wouldn't get smashed. "You could have a very valuable property, Leonard. I'd hate it if someone were to steal it from you."

"That won't happen." I wanted to get over to Mack and watch the race. "I have a patent application or something."

"In your name? Those things are very technical. Are you sure it's been done correctly?"

"I don't know."

"Why don't you let me look at it?" she asked. "I'm an attorney."

"Gosh. Thanks." It was nice of her to be so interested in me, I thought.

"I represent inventors and make very very sure no one takes advantage of them."

Mack watched us out of the corner of his eye. "You do?" I asked her.

The big guy, the battleship, steamed up and butted in. "Marvelous race. Marvelous show. Your flycycle is performing splendidly. J. Bullobear, young man." He grabbed my hand and started shaking it. "Pleased to meet you."

"*I* was talking to him!" the woman lawyer said. "That's very rude!"

Bullobear didn't seem to notice her. "*Spyro's Gyro* is down, Leonard. It's between your flycycle and that tri-winged thing. Let's watch it together, shall we?" His arm was as big as King Kong's and it wrapped around my shoulder.

"Oh no you don't!" Patricia Truesdale said. She grabbed my arm and started pulling me toward her.

"Mack!" I said.

One instant later, Mack planted himself in front of us. "You okay?" he asked me.

"Of course he's okay!" Bullobear said. "He and I are becoming friends. Aren't we, Leonard?"

It sounded like an order from the principal at school. "I—"

"Let him go," Mack said.

"Pay no attention to this fellow," Bullobear told me as he dragged me toward a TV set. "Your flycycle has certain commercial possibilities and..." Suddenly he jumped sideways. "Great Scott!" He let go of me, grabbing his side. "I've been stabbed!" He pulled a thin wire out of his coat, kind of like a big splinter. "Someone pierced me with this!"

"My gosh," I said. It felt like I'd been let out of a stockade. "Who'd do a thing like that?"

Spyro's Gyro landed in a cornfield near Greeley Lake. A TV announcer was there before Chris Spyro had gotten his feet under him. She stuck a microphone in his face. "Mr. Spyro, how do you feel?" she asked.

"Rotten." A gust of wind yanked him and his glider to the left. "Toast, man. My legs are fried."

"Did you ever really think you had a chance?"

"Sure! That's why I got in it."

"But you only managed to go eight miles. Do you feel that you failed?"

He pushed the microphone out of his way. "Get out of my face. Look, I gave it my best shot. Wait'll next year."

"Then you'll be back next year?"

"We all will," he said. "Nobody's gonna finish. Thirty-seven miles is too far."

The camera focused on the TV person. "There you

have it, Polly. A valiant effort from Chris Spyro, and a prediction. They'll all be back next year because no one will finish."

The woman lawyer tapped me on the shoulder. "Leonard, introduce me to your friend," she said.

"Sure. Hey Mack, this is a lawyer I just met."

He turned. "Hello," he said to her and held out his hand. "Mack Rogers."

"Patricia Truesdale," she said, shaking hands. "Nice to meet you. And you are...?"

"Nard and I are partners."

None of us said anything as we watched the race. Julie and the *Tri-Winged Flyer* had made the first turn and were on their way to Eldorado, but the *Tri-Winged Flyer* was ahead. Julie wasn't really headed for Eldorado, in fact. She'd headed east, for Kansas.

"Are you Leonard's guardian *ad litem?*" the lawyer asked Mack.

"What's that?" he asked her.

She laughed. "Obviously not. You know of course that minors can't legally enter into partnerships?"

"I never really thought about it."

"Mack, is Julie okay?" I asked him. "Why's she going so far out of the way?"

"She's being smart," he said. "If she doesn't get too high."

"What will happen if she gets too high?" Patricia asked.

"She could build up too much speed in a downward glide," Mack said. "The fabric covering the wing is very light. It won't take an air speed of more than fifty. If the fabric tears, it could peel off. Then she'd crash."

"Goodness! Have you knowingly subjected that young woman to danger?"

"We had to," Mack said. "To get the weight down low enough to fly."

"Can you trust this 'partner' of yours?" she asked me. "I mean, if he is willing to risk young Julie's very life!"

"She has a parachute," I said. "Mack made her take one."

"I see." She still sounded angry. "And your partnership. I suppose that was his idea too?"

"Sure. He wants to build flycycles after the race."

"Of course he does. He's probably taken out the patent. Am I right?"

I nodded. "I didn't even know you were supposed to."

"*Leonardo's Hand* is at least a mile off the course," the announcer said. "But she's two thousand feet above the ground, which should allow little Julie to glide all the way to Eldorado. Who would you say has the advantage at this point?" she asked the guy standing next to her.

"I like Teddy Frantz and the *Tri-Winged Flyer*," he said. "Notice how he hugs the ground, never more than thirty or forty feet above. The air is thicker there, which helps in a propeller-driven craft. He's moving steadily along in a straight line while that flycycle is all over the map. It's like the tortoise and the hare, you know? The old fable? Give me the tortoise."

"Will either of them finish?"

"Not likely, although Frantz could," he said. "He has tremendous leg strength, another reason you have to give him the advantage. He's raced bicycles in the Tour de France. Not to take anything away from little Julie, who's quite an athlete in her own right, but she's only thirteen."

"You don't know her!" I yelled at the screen.

"Leonard, can we talk privately?" the lady lawyer asked me. She stared at Mack like he was the enemy. "Or will this partner of yours allow it?"

"He doesn't make up my mind," I said.

"I certainly hope not. Let's find some place to sit, all right?"

"I want to watch the race."

"Let me point out some things to you then, Leonard. Have you actually seen the patent application?"

"No."

She glanced at Mack. "The likelihood is it isn't even in your name. Am I right, Mr. Rogers?"

"You're wrong. It's in Nard's name."

"Nard? Is that a nickname?" she asked me. I nodded. "And you're very good friends, I'm sure?"

"Like I said, we're partners," I told her.

"And your partner, Mr. Rogers, drew up the agreement between you?"

That made no sense to me. "I didn't know you could draw agreements. All we did is talk about it."

"She means is our agreement in writing," Mack said.

"Do you mind telling me what you've agreed to Leonard?"

"Why?"

"Because so often an inventor gets nothing for his idea."

I'd figured her out by this time. "How much should the inventor get?"

She stared at Mack. "At least one third of any royalties."

"'Royalties' is like a share of the profits?"

"Yes."

"Wow," I said, opening my eyes wide. "That's a lot."

"Forty percent would be more like it," she told me. "He should also pay you an advance, I'd think at least thirty thousand dollars."

"No kidding."

"Nard honey, the point is this. You need an agent, someone who will represent *you* in your dealings with Mr. Rogers."

"I do?"

"Your agreement. Has it even approached what I've told you you're entitled to?"

"It's way better than that," I said. "He wants to give me half the profits."

"Well. That could be very generous, perhaps, depending on how he defines profits. What about an advance?"

"If we win the race? I get all of it."

"She's catching up," the announcer said. "Frantz has made the turn over Eldorado Park, but *Leonardo's Hand* is going much faster. Don't you agree, Bucky?"

The expert's name was Bucky. "She could get lucky," Bucky said.

"Nard, please listen to me," the lady lawyer said, standing in front of me so it was hard not to. "You are *not* bound to your so-called partner in any way. You are a minor and the law protects minors, even from themselves."

"It does?"

"I firmly believe you need protection. I've had experience in these matters and the probability is, your partner has taken advantage of you. You won't know until an experienced person looks carefully into your deal."

"Didn't you say I could break my agreement any time I want to?" I asked her.

"I'm not sure I said that, but it's true. You can."

"Then *he's* the one who needs protection."

"Nard." She dropped on her knee, so I had to look down at her. "I want to help you, to represent you, to make sure you get the very best deal there is for your invention."

I looked at Mack, who had a skeptical smile on his face. "She's talking about money, isn't she?"

"I am, Nard. Oodles and oodles. More than you can imagine."

"Do you have one of those cards with your name and telephone number on it?" I asked her.

"Yes!" She pulled one out of the air like a magician and stood up. "You be sure and call as soon as you can."

I felt great. Now I could prove something to Mack. "I won't be calling," I said. "Mack decides those things." I gave the card to Mack. "If he thinks we need a lawyer, he'll give you a call."

Twenty-Eight

The *Tri-Winged Flyer* had slowed down! Part of it was the wind, which blew in Teddy Frantz's face. When the screen showed his expression, you could tell he didn't have much left in him. He was dying.

Someone outside the tent yelled inside. "You can see them!" he hollered. "They're less than three miles away!"

Everybody ran outside. Cars streamed back to Table Mountain, which started looking like a big parking lot again. "Keep this area clear!" some attendants yelled as Mack and I headed for the south edge.

"Look, Mack! There she is!"

"Nard! Mack! Git over here!" someone yelled.

It was Anna. She and Farley were right next to the edge. "Look up there!" Farley called out. "That's my daughter up there!" he told anyone who'd listen. "She's flyin' in the sky like a bird. That's my little Julie up there and she's flyin'!"

It was so cool. The *Tri-Winged Flyer* chugged along near the ground like a flat-bottomed rowboat going up a stream, while Julie, way high in the sky, glided for the finish line.

I ran to the edge to see better. The *Tri-Winged Flyer* was in front, but had to climb a hundred feet in the air! "Hurry up, Julie!" Except she couldn't go any faster without... I heard a tearing sound. "Julie! Look out!"

The top sail of the left wing started tearing. A piece lifted in the air like a flag, and Julie was three hundred feet above the ground. *Leonardo's Hand* tilted and slowed, then started crisscrossing and dropping like a falling leaf. "Bail out, Julie!"

She wouldn't bail out. She started pedaling like crazy to keep from dropping too fast.

I heard a thud. It was Teddy Frantz in the *Tri-Winged Flyer*, who ran into the mesa...

"She's done it!" a huge voice boomed, right behind me. "Will you look at that!"

It was Glen Turner, the billionaire, bashing me on the back.

"Young man, your flycycle has won! Congratulations!"

Leonardo's Hand wasn't the sleek-looking bird she'd been at takeoff. But Julie had twisted and tweaked and gotten her over the runway. The guards kept people back, but let Mack and me through. We ran to her. She sagged the last few feet toward the ground. The wind had stopped, and Julie lit on her feet, stood there for ten seconds, then sat down.

"You did it, girl!" Mack said, unbuckling the harness and lifting the flycycle off her. "You did it!" He was crying. "Talk about a champ!"

"Where's Teddy?" she asked, not able to move yet.

"Cracked up." I grinned at her, thinking she'd be glad to know what happened to him. "He ran into the mesa."

"Did he really?" She sounded disappointed.

What made her so sad? "That's why you won, Julie."

"He tried so hard," Julie said. Tears leaked down her cheeks, but she was too tired to cry. "I wish both of us had."

I rode with Mack. Vinci hid out in the back seat of Mack's car. We drove into the yard by the farmhouse first. Anna, Julie, and Farley were right behind us in the pickup.

Two Bergen County Sheriffs' units were parked in the yard, waiting for us! A big detective opened the door for me. "Am I under arrest again?"

"Not this time," he said, grinning at me. "Hey. We watched the finish on TV. What a race!"

Anna jumped out of the truck. "Did you catch them?" she asked a woman officer. I recognized her as the person in that swat team who'd been nice to me.

"Yes," she said, "but they won't tell us their names. Someone will have to identify them for us."

Anna and I walked over to the patrol cars. Erik sat in the back seat of the first one with handcuffs on, hiding his face. Mikey and Fish were in the other one. Fish was crying. "That's Erik Robinson," I said. "The guy with black hair is Mikey. The one who's crying is Fish. I don't know their last names."

"When was the last time you saw them, Nard?" she asked, taking notes.

"That day Farley tried to rob a bank and you made me come out of the house with my hands up. They'd hidden in the root cellar and Erik had a gun. They went in the house, trashed it, and shot at something. We found one of the bullets in the couch, and Anna gave it to you."

She opened the trunk of one of the cars and showed me a pistol that had a cylinder where the bullets go. "Is this the gun he had with him?" she asked.

"I don't know," I said. "It could be."

"Anything else you can tell me?"

"Yes. I'll bet their boat's tied to Anna's dock."

It was. We learned later that the police found a telescope, a laptop computer, and a video camera in the boat. The stuff belonged to a family whose home had been broken into in Bergen Heights.

When Anna gave the bullet we found in the couch to the detectives, they told her they needed the gun. Then a firearms expert could do tests to prove that the bullet in the couch, as well as the bullet found in the dog, had been shot from it. So they worked out a plan to trick the gang into coming back to the farm. Anna and the sheriff's department spread the word that she had three thousand dollars, in cash, hidden in her house. "That was a lie," she said, "but I don't feel bad about it."

On race day, two sheriff's deputies hid in the root cellar and waited. The so-called Bergen Heights Burglars showed up at eleven and were caught inside the house. Erik had the gun in his coat pocket, a detective told us later. It was a .38 calibre revolver he'd bought at a gun show. Tests showed it had definitely fired the bullet in the couch, and probably the one in the dog. "Those boys," he said, "are in a heap of trouble."

Farley didn't go to jail for the rest of his life, which was probably a mistake. His lawyer got him a plea bargain. Farley has to do "community service," where he goes to schools and tells kids about the trouble he's in and that there are better ways to solve problems than robbing banks. It *is* a community service too. He has to take showers on a regular basis.

Erik, Mikey, and Fish got plea bargains too. They were seventeen years old and could have been charged as adults and sent to prison, but the prosecutor thought that would turn them into hardened criminals. So they were sentenced to six months at the Mount View School for Delinquents, and after that, to a regimented juvenile training program, and after that, they'll have to report to a probation officer for three years.

The judge really blasted their parents. "These boys, from Bergen Lake Estates, started by vandalizing a farm in their wealthy suburban area," she said. "The farm was considered an eyesore by many of the homeowners. Their fathers knew what the boys were up to and did nothing to stop them. Instead, they winked at one another, and slapped their sons on the back. Then the vandalism escalated into burglary, a weapon was used, and a dog was shot. If I could send the parents to jail, I would."

Anna paid Mr. Robinson's bank loan off, and won't have to sell the farm to pay for Julie's back operation either. Julie doesn't need one, which the doctors can't explain, even though they try to. They don't understand the improvement in her back. Now they think the problem was the muscles in her back, not her spine. For some reason, the muscles wouldn't relax. Even at night when she slept, they twisted and pulled and tugged her spine into a spiral staircase. "Occasionally one's body acts as though it has a mind of its own," one of them said. "Something must have changed its mind."

Most of the contest money sits in the bank. A third is mine, a third went to Anna to pay her bills, and the other third is Julie's. I practically had to force the shares on

Anna and Julie. I made them take it because it was fair. They had as much to do with winning the contest as I did, I told them, which surprised me. It meant giving good money away.

I paid Mrs. Cousins the twenty-five dollars I owed her, too. At first she wouldn't take it, but I told her the business I'm in with Mack is making me rich. I get two hundred and thirty dollars for each flycycle we sell, and so far we've sold forty-eight! Sometimes she'll call me up just to talk, instead of to do a report. She told me another boy uses my hideout now, but that's okay. I don't think I'll ever need it again.

The big surprise is the neighborhood kids. Some of them came over to tell Anna they weren't all like Erik, Mikey, and Fish. She said she knew that, then asked them if they'd like to help out around the farm! Since then, they've painted the barn and the house, and mended the fence, and learned how to feed the animals and milk Veronica and shear sheep. She pays them with food and hugs and about the best advice a kid can get. She sure can change a kid . . .

Which, I have to admit, she did to me. She taught me there are people, even adults, that you can trust. And money isn't as important as being able to trust someone. I've even gotten to where I can stand Vinci. He still hangs around, keeping Julie's back relaxed and writing stupid notes to me. Like this one:

My dear young obligation and responsibility, with eyes to see but without the wit to open them:

Mankind strangles the earth with roads. Machines that speed along them spew foreign matter into the air, replacing the clean wonderful substance God wished for us to breathe with toxic fumes. And the roads themselves prevent the land from breathing.

Your mission, dear Nard, is to alter this course of destruction. Will you not re-configure, through the exercise of your intellect, these means of transportation that Mankind has cursed himself with?

Open up your eyes, young sir! Who knows? There could be money in it!

Glen Turner just put out the rules for next year's CUTA! contest. Vinci wants to get me in it, naturally. This time, the contest would be a lot different. The big winner has to design a city that doesn't use cars.

I'm thinking about it.